Praise for *SUDDENLY...!* storytelling show and audiobook

Customer review, Waterstones

'A rip-roaring audiobook... non-stop adventure
featuring delicious wordplay'
Kentish Towner

'You rock! I am so encouraged to read more'
Hannah, age 8, Brentwood Children's Literary Festival

'Classic British nonsense. Loved it :)'
Parent, Barnes Children's Literature Festival

'Spellbound from the start... thoroughly entertaining but there's also a
strong educational aspect to the show...
performed with infectious energy and enthusiasm'
Theatre Things

'I love this show, it has inspired me to write my own stories and plays'
Tilly, age 9, Cockpit Theatre

'Amazing! You are such wonderful storytellers. We'll come again and again
until my children outgrow you!'
Parent, Watermill Theatre

'Keeping a school entertained from Reception to Y6 is quite a feat,
but the show had a rapt audience... a real must-see!'
Class teacher, Cheapside Primary

'Fantastic... supported the love of reading and telling stories – perfect for
our book week! All the children absolutely loved the show'
Y6 teacher, Oaklands Primary

To Milo —

Happy reading!

Love Deborah x

William Wood.

SUDDENLY...! and other stories
by Joe Bromley

SUDDENLY...!
adapted from the storytelling show
by Joe Bromley and Willow Nash
Really Big Pants Theatre Company

STUMPED!

SHELVED!

illustrated by Rosie Alabaster

SUDDENLY...! and other stories first published in 2018

Second edition 2018

© Joe Bromley 2018

Illustrations © Rosie Alabaster 2018
www.rosiealabaster.com

ISBN 978 1 9999461 0 4

A CIP catalogue record for this book is available from the British Library

This is a work of fiction. Names, characters, businesses, places, events, locales, and incidents are either the products of the author's imagination or used in a fictitious manner. Any resemblance to actual persons, living or dead, or actual events is entirely coincidental

Printed and bound in Great Britain

Orphans Press Ltd, Arrow Close,
Leominster Enterprise Park, Leominster, Herefordshire HR6 0LD
Tel 01568 612460 www.orphans.co.uk

for my oldies
for beginning my story

for Banners
whose story ended too soon

and for Manuel, Harvey, Nichols, Elsie, Flo,
Dora, Henry and Tilly Peeg –
cats, past and present,
who have purred across these pages
(leaving many a muddy paw print on the way)

Really Big Pants is a theatre company specifically for primary-aged children. We wrote our show, *SUDDENLY...!*, to celebrate and encourage literacy, using recognisable elements of traditional tales (and some really big pants) to inspire and entertain.

When we were approached by Strathmore Publishing to adapt the show into an audiobook, we jumped at the opportunity. You can listen to that story on a good old-fashioned CD player or contact us to find out which cloud it's floating on.

But we mostly got asked if there was a print version. And now there is.

We intended this book to have something for everyone: whether having it read to them; being confident and keen enough to power through in one sitting; or just dipping in and out whilst coming to terms with the craziness of English words and grammar. (Right now we're questioning those semi-colons. See? We get how tricky it all is.)

We also kind of fancied it as a three-course meal. The starter is the adaptation of our show and we hope readers will recognise moments they have seen on stage. Then there are two more adventures for Grandma and Red. The middle story, or the main course, has a more complex structure with parallel timelines for ambitious readers. And for pudding, the final story has a straightforward structure and is short enough to be read in one go.

There are many readers who love a knotty plot but struggle with the form. After researching dyslexia-friendly fonts, we have chosen a large typeface printed on off white paper, used extra spacing and not justified the margins – with the aim of making our stories challenging but the physical act of reading as easy as possible.

Happy reading.

Joe and Willow
Really Big Pants

Contents

Contents

Chapter One

"Once upon a...
time for bedtime stories!"
called Grandma, rubbing her
hands together with glee and
bouncing up and down on a
mini trampoline.
"Come on, Red!"

BOING

Red, in her stripy
pyjamas and trusty red
hoodie, hurtled into the room
on her scooter. She loved
bedtime stories with Grandma.
As well as reading them from a
book, they made up their own
too. Stories that had a beginning,
a middle and an end, goodies
and baddies, things that went
right, things that went wrong, and lots of 'suddenlies'!
And people didn't necessarily live happily *ever* after,
but they always tried their best.

Red headed straight to the bookcase. "Which
story will it be tonight, Grandma? Cinderella?" she
asked.

"Pah, no, not that wishy-washy girl, waiting for a prince, a pumpkin and a fairy godmother to make her happy," scoffed Grandma, bouncing ever higher.

"Snow White?" wondered Red, browsing the packed shelves.

"With all those men to cook and clean for? What kind of a story is that?!"

Red held a book up. "Sleeping Beauty?"

"Surrounded by brambles and reliant on a prince to stop her snoring? I think not!" With an indignant spring, Grandma vaulted clean over the sofa and landed on a colossal cushion. Reaching underneath, she pulled out a well-thumbed paperback and waved it at Red.

"How about a woman with some gumption? Amelia Earhart? Queen Elizabeth I? A cartoon explorer? When I was a suffragette with Mrs Pankhurst, we would always –"

Suddenly, there was a loud knock at the door.

"Who could that be, at this time?" grumbled Grandma, reluctantly putting the book down. She patted her huge amount of hair, piled precariously high on her head and held together with a myriad of pins, numerous rollers, some bits of ivy and a few twigs (and very possibly a snack from earlier), then smoothed down her nightshirt and made her way to the front door. The front door of an amazing treehouse, where Red and Grandma lived, on the outskirts of an enchanted wood.

She peered out into the night through a random porthole window. And spotted her neighbour outside, the wily Mr Wolfe. Clutching a bag of money. Grandma sighed. "Not again. He's always coming round, huffing and puffing and threatening to blow this house down," she muttered. "What does he want now?"

She opened the door and Mr Wolfe stepped inside, scratching his ear.

"Evenin', Grandma, lookin' lovely as ever," he

said, with a wolfish grin. "I'll cut to the chase. What it is, Grandma, is my missus has sent me round to have a word –"

"Ah yes, I heard you recently got married again, Mr Wolfe," she interrupted. "How is your new wife settling in with you and your son?"

"Oh yeah, she's a wicked stepmother. Thing is though, she ain't happy about this tree. I don't mind yer quirky little house. After all, we had that old woman who lived in a shoe just down the road. But 'er indoors says your ancient oak is an 'orrible sludge-green colour and it don't match her purple hair, so it's got to go. How much do yer want for it?" Mr Wolfe jiggled his bag of gold coins.

Grandma fixed him with a stern stare. "Tell me, when you say 'got to go', are you in fact suggesting we chop this tree down?"

"Yeah, that's right, G-ma," he replied. "I knew you'd see sense. You could settle into a nice little bungalow."

Grandma's hair bristled. "Mr Wolfe. This isn't just my home. And my granddaughter's home. And home to birds, squirrels, hedgehogs, and a stray polar bear."

She began to get more animated as she

defended nature and her
beloved treehouse. "It is
also providing the air that
we breathe in. Cleaning
the air that we breathe out.
Giving shade on sunny days.
Shelter on rainy days.
And its roots help prevent
flooding and mudslides.
What price would you put on that,
Mr Wolfe?" she finished with a flourish, as her hair
sent out a shower of sparks.

    Alas, Mr Wolfe wasn't a big fan of nature and
didn't quite understand. He put his arm round her,
thinking it would charm his neighbour. "Ah, you drive
a hard bargain, Grandma, but I respect you for it. I'm
in the tree business myself after all, got 25 acres of
apples and pears growing out the back. 'Wolfie's
Juices. Our money *does* grow on trees.'" He reached
into the bulging bag and lifted out some shiny coins,
in what he imagined was an enticing manner. "Name
your price."

    Grandma was NOT impressed. Rolling up her
sleeves, she took him by the scruff of the neck and
pushed his face right into his money bag. "There is

more to life than money, Mr Wolfe, and spending it on lots and lots of useless stuff!" She gave him a shake and released him.

Mr Wolfe scratched his ears, and tried to regain some composure. "Really? Such as?"

Grandma flung her arms up in the air in frustration. "Flying your kite in the rough winds of May!" she cried. "Paddling at the seaside on a hot summer's day. Rustling through autumn leaves to collect acorns and conkers. Building a snowman with friends – missing that would be bonkers! Or simply try snuggling up with the ones you love for bedtime stories." And with that she turned him round to face the door, took aim, and gave his bottom a mighty kick!

"Goodnight, Mr Wolfe!" she said, pushing him out and closing the door firmly behind him. Grandma heard him howling, and reluctantly phoning his wife to tell her the bad news, as he slunk off into the night with his tail between his legs.

Chapter Two

Meanwhile, back at Mr Wolfe's mansion, Edwin, his spoilt son, was waiting impatiently. He needed help with his homework and he wanted some attention from his father.

"I can't do my homework," whined Edwin, leafing through his school book, blotted with lots of red marks from his teacher. He slowly began to read out what was required of him. *"Make up your own story, tale, fable or legend, and then write it down.* A leg-end? What's a leg-end?" He gave a long groaning howl. "Oh, what do I know about stories? I hate reading and writing! I can't do it – because... because... because... my pencil's broken," he declared, snapping the poor pencil in half. He flung his homework to the ground and stamped his foot in frustration.

But his stepmother was too busy stamping HER foot to notice. Svetlana, the new Mrs Wolfe, had not taken the news about Grandma's treehouse well.

"Vaaaat? Vat you mean tree is not for chop? Either that tree goes or I do!" Svetlana imperiously fluffed her already huge purple hairdo up to maximum height and poked Edwin sharply in the shoulder. "Tell that to your father!"

"Well, I would tell him, Svetlana, but I never get a chance to see him! His face is always buried in his phone," retorted Edwin.

Svetlana was not the sympathetic type and fell considerably short on maternal instinct. "Vat you complaining about? He's on that phone ordering stuff for us. Vat the matter, you not like stuff? Everybody like stuff. Everybody LOVE stuff, right?"

She began to sing. And do a rather alarming little dance.

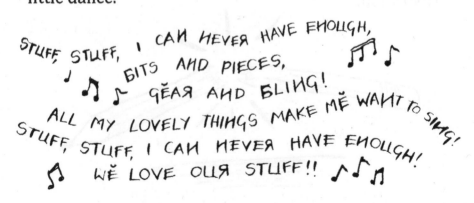

STUFF, STUFF, I CAN NEVER HAVE ENOUGH,
BITS AND PIECES,
GEAR AND BLING!
ALL MY LOVELY THINGS MAKE ME WANT TO SING!
STUFF, STUFF, I CAN NEVER HAVE ENOUGH!
WE LOVE OUR STUFF!!

As the song and strange dance (that had featured several hazardous pirouettes and a lot of arm flapping) came to an end, Svetlana realised she was hugging the curtains and Edwin was watching her, bemused. She shooed him aside dismissively, once more fluffing her mass of hair. "So leave your father alone. And let him order some more stuff," she told her stepson.

Edwin turned away, defeated, and mumbled to himself. "She *is* right, I do love stuff." He thought about his life-sized robots, his own rollercoaster, and fleet of miniature racing cars. "But what I really need is just to be with Dad now and again, and for Dad to be with me."

He gave a deep sigh and reached for his homework. "I'd better get on with this *story*." He slumped down in the corner of the room, behind a large plant pot.

Svetlana was lost in a reverie about stuff, and forgot she was not alone. "At last, my favourite part of day," she said, jiggling with anticipation. "Time to myself with magic mirror!"

On hearing this, Edwin peeped through the fronds of the fern. He saw his stepmother holding aloft an ornate mirror, exactly the size of her face.

And he watched as she gazed into it and uttered the secret password.

"BABUSHKA!"

The mirror shuddered slightly as it came to life. In a low voice, it replied, "Hello, Svetlana."

Svetlana preened and posed and simpered. "Mirror, mirror, in my hand, who's got the best stuff in the land?" she asked it.

The mirror usually answered instantly. But tonight it thought long and hard before stating, "You do indeed have a lot of stuff, Svet, sweetie, it is true. But it is Grandma who has the BEST stuff. Better than you."

Svetlana stiffened. "Vat?? Grandma? Which Grandma?"

"Your old best friend from ballet school in Russia," came the reply.

"*That* Grandma. Why you talking of her?" demanded Svetlana, tossing her hair wildly.

The mirror told her that Grandma lived in the oak treehouse next door.

Svetlana was incredulous. "Grandma lives in that sludge-green tree? Pah! She always liked to be different."

But it got worse. The mirror informed Svetlana

that not only was Grandma her neighbour, but went on to list her best stuff – flying a kite... paddling at the seaside... snuggling up for bedtime stories.

Svetlana stamped her feet, not for the first time that evening. Edwin shrank further behind the plant pot as she began to pace around the room, complaining about how Grandma had had the best stuff when they were children, when they'd been at ballet school together in Russia. And how Big G had shared everything... and then suddenly, how she had stopped sharing.

"Why did she do that, Svetlana?" questioned the mirror, trying to be supportive.

"She said she wanted me to be friends with her for who she was, not for all the lovely stuff she had. She used to be my best friend. Now, mirror, you are my best friend. I even call you Babushka, Russian word for Grandma. And Grandma is my worst enemy." Svetlana sucked her thumb and cuddled the mirror for comfort. And slowly an idea came to her. "But –" out came the thumb – "I will get my revenge. That tree is going, by hook or by crook, along with all her 'best' stuff. Ha! Ha ha! Ha ha ha!"

And with that, Svetlana flounced out of the room, with her tower of purple hair wobbling like a

giant jelly on her head.

Chapter Three

Edwin gathered his thoughts from behind the plant pot. He had a disturbing image in *his* head of his stepmother and his neighbour as ballerinas, prancing around in tutus and trying to balance on tiptoes underneath their immense hairdos, but he shook the unsettling scene from his mind and began to piece together a plan.

It was clear that Svetlana wanted to get rid of Grandma's treehouse. If *he* could get rid of the tree himself, then she would be really happy... and if *she* were happy, then his father would be really happy... with HIM.

"I'll just order some stuff!" he exclaimed. "From the internet!" Edwin scrambled up and grabbed one of his many tablets – just as Mr Wolfe walked past the door, with his face buried in his phone.

"Dad!" he called excitedly. "Dad, listen! I've got a great idea!"

But Mr Wolfe held up a finger. Edwin knew this signal very well. It meant he was supposed to put his own finger on his lip and not speak.

"Not now, son, I'm on the internet," said Mr Wolfe, not looking up from his phone.

Edwin took a chance. "Yes, I know, Dad, but –" he began.

"Not now, son, I'm doing a deal," came the irritated response.

Edwin persisted. "But Dad, could I just –"

"For the last time, Edwin, I'm busy." Finally, Mr Wolfe looked up. But not in a good way. "I'm trying to buy 25 gallons of 'Perky Purple' hair dye to paint that bloomin' tree to match Svetlana's hair." He dialled a number and held the phone to his ear (after scratching it. His ear, not his phone). Edwin watched as his dad strode off placing his order, although there was clearly some confusion over the shades 'Perky Purple' and 'Pooey Purple' with the salesman.

Despondently, Edwin realised he'd have to get rid of the tree by himself. And that he'd better act fast before all that hair dye arrived. He thought for a moment and then carefully intoned 'How to get rid of a sludge-green tree' into the speakerphone on his tablet. He scrolled through a lot of ridiculous options (and a few quite sensible ones), until he reached one that caught his eye.

"*Genies R Us*," he read. "*Your wish is our command! Free lamp with every purchase.*" That sealed the deal. Edwin couldn't resist stuff. He pressed *Add to basket* and smirked at the satisfying ping of confirmation.

And then he settled down by the front door to wait. Impatiently.

Chapter Four

Suddenly, the doorbell rang.

Edwin yanked the door open, grabbed the parcel from the delivery person's hands and slammed the door shut, without a word of thanks.

He tore off the huge bow that held the box shut. And there on a glittery bed of sequins lay a sparkling golden lamp. Edwin grasped it, throwing the box aside. With a triumphant grin, and the certainty that he knew what he was doing (having seen it on television), he held it high and began to rub.

And rub.

And rub.

He looked around, confused. "Nothing's happened. It's not working!" complained the boy. He rubbed each side. He rubbed the lid. He rubbed underneath. He even tried rubbing the box. And that's when he spotted the instructions, and groaned. MORE READING!

```
INSTRUCTIONS!
 • Stretch up high and touch the sky.
 • Bend down low and touch your toes.
•Clap your hands, and stamp your feet.
•Wiggle your bottom to the genie beat.
```

Edwin followed each order, giving his bottom an extra
wiggle for good measure. Then he rubbed the lamp
again. And screamed! The lamp had scratched his
hand, all the way along his palm!

"Ow!" he cried. "What was that?" He inspected
the lamp carefully. There was a crack down the side!
How had that got there? How troublesome all this
was! Why wouldn't it just work? Why was he having
to do all this by himself? Just as he was thinking
about giving up and going to bed, the lamp began to
judder.

Edwin watched as it quaked and shook and
became rather hot. Still no sign of a genie though. He
gingerly took the lid off.

Nothing.

He peered inside.

Still nothing.

That's it, he decided. I've had enough. His mind turned to his stomach and thoughts of toast with a lot of jam on top. He stomped towards the door, but had only managed three steps before the biggest genie imaginable burst from the lamp!

Edwin fell backwards against an ornamental statue of Svetlana in an unfortunate ballet pose, nearly knocking it over. What a fright! The gigantic genie hovered silently above him. Oh, he was massive! Huge! Bigger than he had appeared in the advert, that's for sure. And for some reason, he was dressed as a tennis player and swinging a racquet, which was most off-putting.

Edwin swallowed hard, twice, and thought back to what he had read in that advert. *Your wish is our command...*

Summoning up his courage, Edwin straightened himself to his full height (not very high). He cleared his throat and said, as imperiously as he could manage, "Genie, I command you to chop down a tree!"

Instantly, an axe replaced the racquet...

... and the tennis outfit turned into a ball gown.

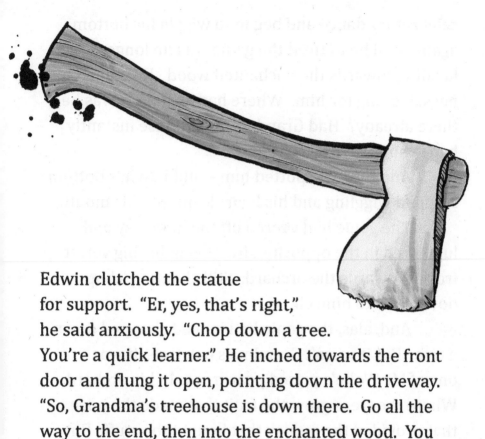

Edwin clutched the statue
for support. "Er, yes, that's right,"
he said anxiously. "Chop down a tree.
You're a quick learner." He inched towards the front
door and flung it open, pointing down the driveway.
"So, Grandma's treehouse is down there. Go all the
way to the end, then into the enchanted wood. You
can't miss it."

Edwin shrank back and heaved a sigh of relief
as the genie squeezed past him and eased its bulk out
through the front door, swinging the axe and chanting
'chop down tree' over and over.

Wow, thought Edwin, that was easy. He'd
solved the problem and his dad was going to be
really pleased with him. He considered doing a little

celebratory dance and began to wiggle his bottom again, until he noticed the genie was no longer heading towards the enchanted wood. He craned his neck, looking for him. Where had he gone? Was he there already? Had Grandma's treehouse instantly been chopped down?

And then he spotted him – and Edwin's bottom stopped wiggling and his heart leapt into his mouth.

The genie had veered off the driveway and lumbered in the opposite direction in his big velvet frock. Towards the orchard. Still chanting 'chop down tree' to himself.

And, alas, the genie had indeed chopped down a tree. But it wasn't Grandma's oak tree. It was one of Mr Wolfe's prized pear trees. In his orchard. Where the trees grew the fruit that made the juice that provided the money that bought the stuff. But the genie didn't stop there. He began chopping down ALL the trees in the orchard.

Edwin gasped. This was a disaster!

"Genie, stop! Stop!" he yelled.

The genie kept chopping.

"I *command* you to stop!!"

Down came another tree.

"Oh, Genie! I wish you'd stoppp!" he pleaded,

wringing his hands. He ran back inside to fetch the lamp. And then realised – the crack! The genie was faulty! Edwin COULDN'T stop him.

He slumped down on the doorstep. He knew he needed help. He also knew he couldn't tell Svetlana. And he certainly couldn't tell his dad. How he wished he had a friend.

Who could help him?

And then it came to him. Red. Red! Yes! She'd know what to do. He jumped up, clutching the lamp, and dashed off, as fast as he could run. Down the driveway he raced, past the fountain with yet another statue of Svetlana in it (this one sprayed water out of her hair), all the way to the end, into the enchanted wood, which he'd always found a bit spooky. Trees loomed above him and branches clawed at his dressing gown. But he had to get to the treehouse! On and on he ran, feeling like his heart would burst.

At last he reached the strange little dwelling. There was a light on in the window.

And for the second time that evening, a member of the Wolfe family knocked loudly on Grandma's door.

Chapter Five

Edwin's knees trembled as he wheezed and tried to get his breath back. He heard a bolt slide back from inside and the door opened. Red!

The young girl yawned, snuggling deeper into her hoodie. "Edwin! What are you doing here? It's really late," she said.

Edwin, panting heavily, held up the lamp.

"Oh, you bought a genie?" she deduced.

He stretched his arms out wide to illustrate the size of it.

"A really big one?"

Edwin nodded, still unable to speak, and then mimed chopping down a tree.

"You told him to make you a banana split sundae?" Red guessed.

He shook his head, and urgently mimed the action again.

"Ah, you told him to chop down a tree?" she asked.

Edwin guiltily indicated the very tree they were standing in.

"*This* tree?!" Red spluttered. "Our home?! Edwin!"

Still panting and wishing he did more PE at school so he'd be fitter and not so out of breath from a little bit of exercise, he desperately tapped the crack in the lamp.

Red peered at it closely. "Hmmm... is this genie faulty?"

Edwin pointed behind him.

"Is he chopping down all the trees in your orchard?! Serves you right!"

Then Edwin signalled from the orchard to the spot where they were standing.

"But he's coming this way?!" Red gasped. "EDWIN!"

Suddenly, Grandma appeared.

"Catch your breath, Edwin, there's not a minute to lose," she said. "We're going to need a very powerful spell from a very special spell book."

With that, Grandma reached up and started rummaging through her hairdo. Edwin watched in astonishment as she delved deeper and deeper. Soon she was up to her elbows in there. Then she gave a cry of triumph and a tiny battered book emerged from the tangles. It seemed to glow with a strange energy.

"My spell book," said Grandma, with pride.

"This was given to me by my good friend, Roald Dahl. We flew together in the RAF during World War II."

She skimmed through the contents pages. *"Trolls. Potions. Cauldrons,"* she read. "It will be quicker if I look in the index at the back." She flipped the pages until she found what she was looking for and gave a cry. *"How to get a faulty genie back into its lamp. Page 152.* Here we go." Reaching the correct page, she scanned the spell, nodding and murmuring to herself. Then she stopped. And drew herself up.

"Red, you and Edwin will need to collect three

things by midnight," she said. "Or there'll be no stopping this genie... ever."

Edwin practically fainted.

But Red said excitedly, "Three things. Like a treasure hunt, Grandma?"

"Indeed," replied Grandma, "but a very dangerous one. One that will require the ABC! To be a) adventurous, b) brave and c) courageous! And to not be afraid of scraping your knee," she referred back to the book, "or of bad smells." Then Grandma plucked a small red star with writing engraved on it from the spell book. She read out:

Soar into the tree-tops, way up high.
Find the nest built in the sky.
You must ask for an egg from a bird of paradise.
Make sure you thank her and be nice.

The first clue!

"I'm on it, Grandma," said Red. "Let's do this thing! I'll get the shopping bag so we don't have to ask for a plastic one."

"Good girl." Grandma reached back into her

hair for another rummage. She removed a well-worn
long white glove with glittering tassels dangling from
the fingertips. "This is your great great-uncle's Go
Glove and it will transport you." She handed it to Red
and then plunged back into her tresses, scattering
hairpins. She withdrew a battered watch on a long
piece of string and hung it round Red's neck. "And
this is my watch so you can keep an eye on the time.
Remember, be back before midnight!" She searched
her mane once more and pulled out a sandwich.

"And what's that?" Edwin asked feebly.

"It's a sandwich, dear," said Grandma, and
took a large bite. "Now off you go. Good luck!" She
saluted the children and vanished.

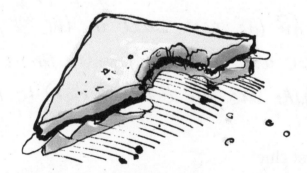

"Thanks, Grandma. And don't worry, we will be back
before midnight," said Red, turning her attention to
the glove.

This evening was getting increasingly alarming for Edwin, and he wished he had a sandwich of his own. He wondered how Grandma had disappeared into thin air, and whether she'd be back with extra food. Then he realised Red had been repeating Grandma's ABC, whilst pulling the glove onto her right hand. It reached all the way up to her elbow.

"Eh? What are you on about? I wasn't listening. Did you say advent calendar –"

But before he could finish his sentence, Red had shouted, "Go, glove!" and spun her arm round, with the tassels flying in all directions and nearly hitting him in the face. His indignation turned to astonishment as, in the blink of an eye, they had been transported up and out of the treehouse, and had landed far far away in a rainforest! But not on the ground – up in the treetops! And not *safely* in the treetops, but on a tightrope – strung between two trees!

Chapter Six

"Wooah," cried Edwin, clutching Red and nearly tipping them both off. "What are we doing up here?!"

"The Go Glove! We're in the rainforest, high up in the treetops," said Red, hurriedly steadying herself and Edwin. "We've got to balance along this tightrope until we reach the bird's nest. It's over there! Follow me."

Edwin could not believe this was happening. But as he saw all the trees around him and heard

the strange exotic sounds of the rainforest, he thought about the genie, out of control in his father's orchard (in a velvet ball gown) and relentlessly chopping down their fruit trees. He took a deep breath and inched after Red. Across they went,
> slowly,
>> slowly,
>>> slowly...
until Edwin wobbled. "Wooah-woaaahahhah-wooaaaaahhhhh!!" He tried to grab Red's hoodie but missed, catching the tassels from the Go Glove in his hand instead. He wrenched at them to save himself, but too late!

Off they both fell –

DOWN

DOWN

DOWN

DOWN

– through the branches, falling,
                    falling,
                        falling.
    Edwin closed his eyes and thought about how
he'd miss his robots, and his rollercoaster... and his
dad...

He landed in the bird's huge nest.

"Oh," he said. "Surprisingly soft, this nest." He lay there for a moment, relaxing. Until he heard the muffled voice of Red beneath him.

"Edwin, you're squashing me."

"Ah, that's why it was soft. Oops," he said, getting up and looking around. "Right, where's this bird then?" He turned and came face to face with a rather bedraggled creature, flapping her wings and glaring at him with beady eyes. He stepped back in surprise as she landed at his feet. "Oh! Er, are you a bird of paradise?" The bird nodded her head. "Good. Lay an egg then."

The bird gave him a haughty look and shook her tail feathers.

"Here, are you laying one?" he asked. She considered him for a moment and seemed to wink at Red, before beckoning him closer. Edwin leaned down, expectantly. The bird waited until he drew level with her and was as close as he could possibly be... and then blew a raspberry, right in his face! She did a little birdie hop of pleasure, as Red laughed.

Edwin wiped his face with his handkerchief. "Euuugh, yuk! Talk about rude! What's the matter with her, why won't she lay an egg?"

"Have you ever heard of manners, Edwin?" Red asked.

"Manners?" he said, racking his brains.

"Yes," she answered. "Please, thank you, sorry, all the basics. They get you a lot further in life, you know, than being rude. And the clue even *told* us to thank her and be nice."

"Oh. Right. Why didn't you remind me earlier," he sulked.

"Well, perhaps it's good for you to learn these things. Why don't you try again?" Red nudged him towards the bird, still perched nearby.

Edwin regarded the scruffy creature, who resolutely ignored him. He didn't really want to try again, but he knew they didn't have much time. He cleared his throat. "Erm, excuse me, Miss. *Please* will you lay an egg for me?"

The bird slowly turned and contemplated him. Edwin took a step back, in case she was about to blow another raspberry. But instead, she nodded elegantly and ruffled her feathers. Waggling her tail, she flew up and landed on Edwin's outstretched hands. He hardly dared to breathe... as she panted slightly, crossed her eyes, gave a little shudder... and laid an egg.

The bird fluttered to his shoulder, looking very pleased with herself. Edwin turned the egg over and over in his hands. What an incredible thing! It was all the colours of the rainbow with swirls and patterns running through it. He held it up to show Red.

"Red, Red, we've got it! An egg from a bird of paradise!" And then he thought for a moment, and turned to his new feathered friend. "Thank you," he said, meaning it. She nuzzled into him delightedly.

"Well done, Edwin! Look how important manners are!" said Red, checking the watch around her neck. "But we've got to hurry up, we need to look for the next clue. Remember, we have to find three things before midnight to stop that genie. And it's already eleven o'clock!"

They both began to hunt for the clue, searching the nest and their surroundings, with increasing urgency. Until the bird nibbled on Edwin's ear.

"Hey, stop that, it tickles!" he laughed. The bird was pointing her beak towards the egg that Edwin still cradled. Could she be telling him to look inside it? Red and Edwin carefully examined the egg and realised they could open it without damaging it. And that there WAS a clue inside! Another red star!

"Oh, thank you, thank you," cried Edwin joyfully. He read out the writing on the second clue, hesitating slightly on a few of the more difficult sounds.

Are you ready to go to market? For next you'll need a flying carpet! Find the witch with the hooked nose. Just make sure you don't have a doze...

"A doze?" he said. "I'm not remotely tired. Come on, let's get going."

Red raised her hand with the Go Glove on it. And then gasped in horror. All the magic tassels had been torn off. The fingertips were bare.

"Edwin! The Go Glove is ruined!" The little girl realised it must have happened when Edwin had desperately clawed at it as they had fallen through the trees off the tightrope.

"It wasn't my fault!" shouted Edwin, quickly denying any responsibility. "I didn't do it!" He looked around wildly for someone else to blame. He even wondered if he could suggest the bird had eaten the tassels, but she was watching him again with her beady eyes.

Red sank to the ground in despair. How would they get to the market? And how would they ever get back home? If they didn't get all the ingredients for Grandma to do her spell, then the genie was going to chop down their treehouse, and then ALL the trees in the world.

A silence fell. Edwin couldn't think what to say. He knew deep down this *was* his fault; in fact, the whole thing was his fault. But how could he comfort Red? Would manners help? Tentatively, he reached out and squeezed her hand.

"I'm really sorry, Red," he whispered, genuinely meaning it.

The bird cocked her head at this. She once more nibbled on Edwin's ear. And then did the most astonishing thing. She left Edwin's shoulder, flapping her wings, and hovered over the children. As they looked up, her wings grew and grew, until they were enormous, like a plane. The trees around them began to sway in the draught she created.

Red scrambled to her feet. "This magnificent bird's going to fly us to the market!" she called, above the sound of the beating wings. "How wonderful! Quick, jump on!"

And Red was right. Clutching her bag with the egg safely inside, she took hold of the left wing and swung herself up on the bird's now huge back. Edwin, gulping, took hold of the right wing and did the same. There was no time to speak because as soon as they were both holding on, the bird surged upwards, taking them out of the rainforest and far above the land.

They glided and soared, until Edwin dared to open his eyes, and when he did, he saw the market beneath them. "Down there! The market!" he pointed, and they swooped towards it.

"We're coming in to land," shouted Red, as the bird began to shrink back to her normal size, rapidly getting smaller and smaller. Red knew that soon there would be no space left for them to sit, and they had to jump. Off she went, with a whoop, and landed safely, rolling over and over.

Edwin waited until the very last possible moment, when the bird was practically smaller than he was and squawking at him. He thought it safest to close his eyes again. Down he went... and couldn't believe his luck – another comfy landing. Right on top of Red.

They both lay there, catching their breath, and waved goodbye to the intrepid bird who was flying away, free of her burden, and heading back to her nest.

"Thank you!" they called gratefully.

Edwin stood up, and took in their new surroundings. Stuff! Stuff! Stuff everywhere!

Chapter Seven

As Red dusted herself down, she watched Edwin gawping greedily at everything in the market.

"Don't even think about getting any more 'stuff', Edwin. Step away from the stuff. We are looking for a flying carpet." And with that, she began to search the stalls.

Edwin didn't notice. He was gazing at the magic beans. And the crystal balls. And wondering if there was a food stall somewhere in all the hustle and bustle.

And then he spied something he'd wanted for a long, long time – a spinning wheel! He'd always wanted to touch one, and now, here one was right in front of him, all shiny and tempting. He reached his finger out, closer,
  closer,
    closer...

"Ow!" he cried. "That's really sharp!" Edwin had pricked his finger. And suddenly he could barely keep his eyes open. "I feel really sleepy," he yawned. "I'll just have a quick doze."

He curled up on the ground and fell fast asleep. Red was fending off pushy pixies who were selling invisible doughnuts on a stall two rows up, and hadn't noticed. So there was no-one to look out for Edwin as suddenly a witch loomed over him. A witch with a hooked nose.

"Kids!" she hissed at the snoring boy. "Always touching stuff they're not supposed to. Now, any earwax here? Toenail clippings? No? Ah – look – just what I need." There was a little bit of snot dripping from the sleeping child's runny nose. She bent down to collect it, but she was a rather clumsy witch, and the nose took quite a bashing.

Edwin stirred and slowly sat up, stretching. He opened his eyes – nearly jabbing one out on the hooked nose right in front of him! "Aaarghh, you're not Red!"

"Well spotted, my dear," came the sarcastic reply.

What was that rolled up under the witch's arm? "Is that a flying carpet?" he asked, jumping up.

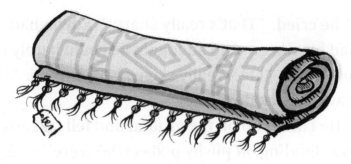

"Might be. Why? Do you want it?"

Edwin held his hands out expectantly, as only a spoilt child can. "Correct, crone. Hand it over!"

"Oh no no no no no, little boy. You're forgetting something. Would you like me to turn you into a giraffe?" tutted the witch.

What was Edwin forgetting? He tried to remember, but was distracted by the thought of being a giraffe, a rather appealing animal, and was weighing up the pros and cons of having a really long neck and excellent eyelashes, when the witch jabbed him with her elbow.

"Oh yes, manners!" he said hastily. "Please, thank you, sorry, pardon, excuse me!"

"Please will do. But what will you give me in return?"

Edwin frantically searched through the pockets of his dressing gown; finding only his handkerchief, a crumpled sweet wrapper, leaves from the rainforest...

he had nothing of value to offer her. "I haven't got anything!" he cried.

But the witch was gazing at the handkerchief. "How snotty is that?" she asked.

Edwin examined it. It wasn't *that* snotty. But suddenly, his nose began to tickle. Oh no, he was going to sneeze!

An — aaah — aaah — aaaachoooo!

He blew his nose, noisily, then regarded the hankie. "It's REALLY snotty."

The witch grabbed it, delighted. "Perfect! Just what I need for my 'learn how to spell' spell. Now I'll be able to enter the Flappington Library Short Story Competition, and I do so love stories." She held out the carpet, gave a loud cackle and twitched her hooked nose. Roller skates appeared on her feet.

bbling and clutching at stalls, and
lling. "Coming through!" Her voice
distance. "C O M M, no, that's not
.. M, careful, look out..."
Edwin couldn't believe it. They had the egg
from the bird of paradise, and now a flying carpet
– they just needed to find one more thing! Which
meant they had to look for one more clue.

He held the carpet up like a telescope,
intending to search the market. At the other end, an
eye looked back at him, unblinking. Red!

"Well done, Edwin," she said. "Try unrolling the
carpet."

Why hadn't he thought of that? And why
was Red licking her lips? Had she eaten something
without him?! He was about to ask her when she
took the carpet and unrolled it... and another red
star tumbled out. The third clue! He snatched it up.
Could he face any more reading? Red discreetly took
it from him, and read it out herself.

You need a mirror, make sure it's magic,
hurry, before this tale turns tragic.
It must belong to a wicked stepmother.
For as the story goes, it can be no other.

Edwin gulped, as realisation dawned. "I've got a stepmother with a magic mirror," he confessed. "Svetlana."

"The same stepmother who wants our treehouse gone!" said Red.

Edwin seized the watch round her neck. "Talking of trees, look at the time. It's half past eleven, only thirty minutes before midnight! Do you know how to fly one of these things?"

Red studied the carpet that was twitching slightly on the ground. "No, but how hard can it be? Jump on! And hold tight!"

As soon as they were both on the carpet, it bucked and reared and jolted into the air. Edwin closed his eyes and held on to Red for dear life as she expertly steered up and out of the market.

"We're turning left!" she called. "We're turning right! Lean back, Edwin, we're going over some mountains! Whoa, we're going through a tunnnnnnel!"

On and on they flew, all the way back to the enchanted wood. Red spotted Mr Wolfe's orchard beneath them where the genie was still chopping down trees. There were hardly any left.

"Brace yourself, we're coming in to land!" she

shouted, as they veered round a particularly pointy statue of Svetlana.

Edwin, of course, still had his eyes shut. And yet again, Red bore the brunt as he landed on top of her with a whump. He got up and brushed himself down.

"I am really good at these landings. And we're right outside my house. Come on, Red."

As Red rolled up the carpet, she gazed up at the vast mansion, and realised this could be their most dangerous challenge yet. Edwin had gone rather pale. He motioned to her to follow him and they crept inside.

Chapter Eight

Red could not help but stare. Svetlana clearly fancied herself as an interior designer... and she also clearly fancied *herself.* The walls were covered with paintings of her. In some, she posed with minor celebrities. Every now and then, there were pictures of her with Mr Wolfe. None with Edwin though.

There was a trophy cabinet at the top of the grand staircase, and Red stopped to look.

It was full of awards for participating in ballet competitions. She noticed that Svetlana had never actually won any of the competitions.

Still, Grandma had always taught her it was the taking part that counted.

She moved off again and bumped into Edwin, who had halted outside an ornate purple door.

"Ssssh!" He was even paler than before. "This is where she keeps her mirror. You wait here. I'll go and get it." He opened the creaking door, very slowly, and crept inside.

"Edwin!" Red whispered loudly. He froze, and retraced his steps back to her.

"Remember. ABC," she mouthed.

"Oh. Yeah. Thanks, Red." He crept off again, frantically wondering what the ABC was. What had she said it stood for? It all seemed so long ago, back in Grandma's treehouse. Was it something about avocados, beans, cauliflowers? His stomach rumbled slightly at the thought of food. WHY hadn't he packed a snack?

And then he heard another rumbling... something much louder than his stomach.

The sound of snoring.

In the dim light, he could make out his stepmother, fast asleep on a plush chaise longue. Holding something tight to her chest. Holding the *mirror* tight to her chest. The magic mirror that he needed for Grandma's spell. How would he get it? He began to sweat and wished for the billionth time that he had not ordered that genie.

Suddenly, Svetlana snorted and burped and started to talk in her sleep. "Grandma," she mumbled. "Your stuff will never be best stuff!" And she took one hand off the mirror to suck her thumb.

This was Edwin's chance. He carefully began to prise the mirror free from her other hand. Her grip was strong, and his hands were clammy. She stirred and muttered, but did not wake. One last finger curled round the handle... Edwin gave the mirror a final tug, and it came free.

He had it! He made a dash for the door.

Red was waiting outside, anxiously looking at the watch round her neck. There were only fifteen minutes left before midnight. Edwin held up the mirror, ecstatically. They clutched each other and began to jump up and down (very quietly). They'd done it!

Suddenly, the door burst open. Svetlana stood there, eyes flashing, and foaming at the mouth.

"Aaaaaaaaarghh!" screamed both children.

They turned to run, but Svetlana reached out and caught hold of Red's hoodie. Quickly, the little girl wriggled out of her beloved garment, leaving it in Svetlana's grasping clutches. They fled down the stairs as she shrieked at them, simultaneously shaking her fist and holding the hoodie away from her in disdain.

"To the scooters!" cried Edwin. They grabbed two from his vast collection and scooted back to the treehouse, with only minutes to spare!

Chapter Nine

They flew in through the door.

"Grandma!" yelled Red. "We're back. We did it! We got all the ingredients."

And then Edwin – and even Red – stopped and did a double take. Grandma was wearing some REALLY BIG PANTS over her nightshirt!

She looked like a very odd yet rather glorious superhero. She had dragged a huge trunk into the middle of the room. There was a strange bubbling sound coming from it and every so often something popped, like a firecracker. The trunk was glowing and there seemed to be a lot of goo spilling out.

"Well done, both of you. Time to get that genie back in the lamp. In with the ingredients!"

Red hurled the flying carpet into the trunk. The goo spluttered and spat.

Edwin threw in the egg from the bird of paradise. Flashes of light shot up to the ceiling.

Grandma added the mirror. A wild groaning and gurgling filled the room.

Then Grandma stuck her finger in the mixture and tasted it. She winced and went cross-eyed. "It's missing something. Red, fetch me some droppings from a blue rabbit. Count sixteen and make sure they're perfectly square."

"I'm on it, Grandma. Come on, Edwin." Red headed off, with Edwin following. "Snowy will be on the climbing frame. You can't get him off it."

Grandma turned back to the spell she had been preparing. She knew they didn't have long and that this would be their only chance to stop that genie. What would happen if they missed the midnight deadline and the genie chopped down their treehouse? She knew he would keep going until he'd chopped down all the trees in the world. And where would the world be without trees?

She shuddered to think... and then stiffened.

For the third time that evening, a member of the Wolfe family was at the door – and this one hadn't bothered to knock.

Chapter Ten

Svetlana stood behind Grandma, dangling Red's hoodie from her fingertips. "Grandma," she crowed. "Not so fast. So *this* is your best stuff?" She looked around with scorn.

Grandma slowly turned to face her old best friend, after all these years. Both of their huge hairdos began to crackle with electricity: Grandma's grey and natural and tangled with treasure; Svetlana's purple and livid and proud.

"Svetlana, is that you?" said Grandma.

"Yes. You like vat you see? Now *I'm* the one with the best stuff. Better than you, my used-to-be-best friend."

Grandma shook her head in disbelief. "Ah, Svetlana. You haven't changed. Still putting 'stuff' before friendship. Why are you here?"

Svetlana threw the hoodie at Grandma, who caught it and held it close to her heart.

"I am here to get my revenge," cried Svetlana, putting her fists up.

She was here for a fight! Well, thought Grandma, if that's what she wants... she placed the hoodie on a chair and put her fists up too.

And so it began! They danced round the room, throwing punches at each other. Round and round they went, spinning, leaping, whirling; two old friends with years of history between them, enraged and solving nothing. Dodging blow after blow, Grandma caught sight of the cuckoo who lived above the fireplace. It reminded her to look at the clock.

Five minutes before midnight! She put her fists down.

"Not now, Svetlana. There's no time to spare!" she declared.

But Svetlana was not giving up. "No time to spare. No stuff to share!" she shouted, dropping into a karate stance. "Suddenly, you stopped sharing your stuff!" She aimed a kick at Grandma, who deftly caught the foot and gave it a good tickle before letting it go.

"You're right, Svetlana," she said. "I did stop sharing and it felt very lonely. I was wrong. I made a mistake. And I'm sorry for hurting you." She held out her hands in a gesture of peace.

Svetlana grandly batted the gesture away. "You don't hurt me. I learned long ago never to be hurt by anyone."

"But I wanted you to be friends with me for who I was, not the stuff I had," continued Grandma.

Svetlana was unconvinced. "But you always had best stuff. Not so now! Paddling at seaside and building snowmen?! Pah!"

Grandma sighed. Was there any point trying to explain how she shared all the important 'stuff' in her life – her home, her love and her belongings?

It was as if Svetlana had read her mind. She pointed to Grandma's superhero underwear. "Please, keep your really big pants to yourself. Nobody wants to share those. And as for your sludge-green tree of a home, you won't have it to share much longer. I saw on Twitter there's a genie chopping down trees and he's heading this way!"

Grandma turned to the clock. Two minutes to

go!

"Svetlana," she said, "I'm sorry your heart is as hard and cold as a mirror. But I don't have time for this." She plucked the mirror from the trunk, using it to stir the squelchy goo. "Where is Red with those droppings?"

"My mirror!" screamed Svetlana. "I knew it! That mirror belongs to me." And she charged at Grandma, chasing her round and round the trunk, over chairs, under tables, in and out of the fireplace, their hair flying, until they both had to stop to catch their breath. Svetlana snatched one end of the mirror. They tugged it back and forth between them in a fierce battle.

"Let! Go! Now!" she screeched. She tried to slam Grandma's hand against the trunk. But in her fury and exhaustion, she missed and it was the mirror itself that received the fatal blow... shattering it into a thousand pieces. As the shards plummeted into the trunk, sparks flew and a terrible smell filled the room.

Grandma was hurled backwards into the bookcase.

And Svetlana began to convulse uncontrollably. "MY MIRRRRROOOOOR! I'm melting!" she wailed.

Down, down, down she went, oozing into a

frothy puddle as Grandma reached out across the room, and the lost years, to help her. But there was no hope. Within seconds, all that was left of Svetlana was her hair.

The ancient treehouse fell silent. Grandma waited for a moment and then lifted the slightly steaming pile of purple curls from the floor and clasped it to her.

"Oh, Svetlana," she murmured.

Suddenly, Red ran in, calling behind her, "Edwin, you can wash your hands later! Come *on*, one minute left!" She skidded to a halt when she saw Grandma. "Oh! What's happened to Svetlana?"

Grandma put the hair down. "I'll explain later. Midnight is upon us and the genie's coming! In with the droppings!"

Red flung them into the gooey mix.

They all turned to see the genie, huge and ominous, hovering outside the front door; now wearing a wetsuit and a bowler hat... still brandishing the axe.

"Chop down tree," he uttered.

Grandma grabbed the lamp and beckoned Edwin from where he was cowering in the corner.

"Be brave, Edwin," she cried. "Here we go. Everybody, magic fingers!"

Red and Edwin wiggled their fingers in the air for all they were worth. And Grandma began to chant.

> SHARE, CARE, TRY YOUR BEST!
> MIND YOUR MANNERS AND WEAR YOUR VEST!
> IT ALL COMES BACK TO THE ABC!
> BE THE HERO OF YOUR OWN STORY!

She held the lamp up high and snatched the lid off. "Genie – get back in that lamp!" she roared.

The genie resisted to the end, clinging to the door frame, scrabbling at the furniture, shrinking and shrieking until it finally got sucked back into the lamp.

Just as the clock struck midnight.

Chapter Eleven

Yes!" whooped Grandma. Red ran and hugged her.
Grandma drew Edwin in too, who was looking very
pale again.

"We've done it! The genie's back in the lamp."
She tossed it into the infernal goo and, with a strong
sucking sound, the lamp sank to the bottom and
evaporated. Grandma shut the lid.

"That's taken care of him. And our home
stands tall and strong and safe." She hugged the
children tightly. "Well done, both of you. Are you
hungry, dear?" she asked Edwin. His eyes lit up,
hopefully. "Take him to the kitchen, Red, and find him
something nice to eat."

Edwin looked slightly crestfallen that she
wasn't going to conjure something up from her hair,
but on the other hand, he wasn't sure how hygienic it
was to keep food in there.

Grandma turned and surveyed her home. And
the remains of her friend. She gave a deep sigh.

Suddenly, Mr Wolfe arrived. Sheepishly. He
didn't seem to notice the chaos in the room, nor the
really big pants that Grandma was still wearing.

He sat down wearily on the nearest chair and

scratched his ear. "I know it's late, Grandma, but I'm not gonna lie to you: I'm having a bit of a bad day," he said. "I've only got one tree left standing. The rest have been chopped down. My son's disappeared. And me missus is nowhere to be seen. To be honest, I've had enough. But I want you to have the last apple from my orchard." He handed her the shiny red piece of fruit. "I should never have tried to kick you out of your home. I'm sorry."

Grandma graciously accepted the apple. "Thank you, Mr Wolfe. And don't worry, Edwin's fine, he's here with Red. As for your orchard, well, in time, new trees will grow in place of the old ones. As for Svetlana..." She gently passed him the purple remains.

Mr Wolfe gasped. "My Svet! What's happened to her?" He held the hair up and peered through it. "Svetlana, sweetheart, can you hear me? Hello?"

"She will grow back, Mr Wolfe, just like your orchard. But only if you nourish her with your time, sprinkle her with a sense of self-worth, and light her up with your love," said Grandma. She reached into her own hair, one last time, and extracted a tiny glass phial. "And add a drop of this every day."

Mr Wolfe took it and gave it a little shake.

"What's this?"

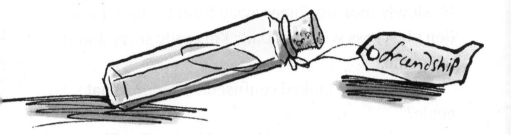

"Friendship. Something we all need," sighed Grandma. "As I said to Rosa Parks on the bus home from bingo one day –"

She stopped. And patted Mr Wolfe's shoulder. "I'll get Edwin," she said, vanishing.

Mr Wolfe hugged the hair to his chest. "Oh my Svet, I promise to do better this time. Don't you worry, I'm going to take care of you. And when you've grown back, you could start your own business selling hair dye. 25 gallons of 'Perky Purple' just arrived. Your favourite colour."

Edwin crept into the room. He gazed at his dad and longed and longed for him. He sighed and put his finger on his lip, the way he always did when his father was busy. "Dad?" he said quietly.

Mr Wolfe gave a howl. "Edwin!" He rushed across the room and lifted his son up in a bear hug.

He hugged him and hugged him and hugged him.

Edwin didn't dare to believe it was happening. He slowly took his finger away from his lip. "Please don't be cross with me, Dad. I'm really sorry about the genie."

Mr Wolfe looked confused. "Genie? What genie?"

"Ah, erm, nothing," he said hurriedly. They settled back into the hug. The best hug ever. What was his father holding though? Edwin turned his head to look and recoiled from the purple mass. "Eww, what's happened to Svetlana?"

"Don't you worry, son," Mr Wolfe reassured him. "I'm gonna nurture you both so we can finally be a proper family. Come on, son, let's go home." He took his hand and they turned to go. "Here, do you need any help with that story homework?"

Edwin smiled. "*Thanks*, Dad, but I've got a great idea for a story now. And I can't wait to write it down! I'll just say goodbye and *thank you* to Red and Grandma."

Mr Wolfe raised an eyebrow. "Really? Well done, son. Yeah, nice. Manners."

Chapter Twelve

Edwin grabbed the hoodie from the chair and ran back to the kitchen. He handed it to Red.

"Thank you," she said, with a smile.

"Thank YOU," he replied. "'Night, Red. You're a real friend."

She held her fist out for him to bump. "'Night, Edwin. Sorry your stepmum melted."

He shrugged. "It's alright. Hopefully she'll be nicer when she grows back."

"Yeah. See ya," she said, slipping her hoodie back on.

Edwin turned to leave. "Oh, and Red? ABC! Avocados, beans, cauliflowers!"

Red laughed. "Edwin! A) Adventurous! B) Brave! C) Courageous! But your version is good too."

She shut the door behind the Wolfes and turned to see Grandma sitting in her favourite armchair with a well-earned cup of tea. Red ran and snuggled in beside her.

"Now, where were we?" she asked, pulling the book out from earlier that they'd been half-sitting on.

"The end," said Grandma. "So, Red, did you like your story...?"

Chapter One

"Grandma!" called Red, leaning out of the window at the top of the treehouse. "Snowy's attacking the postman again!"

Grandma was outside, hanging upside down on the climbing frame in a velour tracksuit. "38 – 39 – 40," she counted, wheezing slightly. "Could you rescue him, dear? I'm just in the middle of my circuit training. Only 60 more crunches to go. 41 – 42 – 43 –"

Quick as a flash, Red ran to the other side of the treehouse and clambered through a trapdoor. This led to a giant slide that went down several floors like a helter-skelter, directly into the garden. Round and round she whizzed, with her trusty red hoodie flying behind her. Beaming from ear to ear, she landed with a

Red scrambled up and ran along the path to where Snowy was savaging the trembling postman.

"Snowy! Down, boy! Behave yourself!" she cried.

"Ow, 'ere, cor blimey, that rabbit ought to be ashamed of itself!" said the indignant postman, brushing down his uniform.

"Sorry, he loves the taste of paper. He just wanted to get at the letters." Red scooped up the small blue rabbit and softly stroked his floppy ears.

"Yes, well, I don't 'alf wish you had a guard dog like most people," the postman grumbled, handing her a stack of mail.

Red cheerfully thanked the postman and wished him a good morning, as he headed back into the enchanted wood that surrounded their home. She wondered what sort of day it was going to be.

Suddenly, Grandma appeared by her side, doing star jumps. "22 – 23 – 24 –" she panted, as her giant hairdo sprang about on her head like a mad jelly. "Nearly time for breakfast, Red. 25 – 26. Just a few more of these. 27 – 28 –" She jumped off down the path, still counting. "And Snowy is nibbling the post, dear. Mind he doesn't eat anything important."

Red hurriedly put down her pet before he could

chomp all the letters and watched him hop off. She went back into the treehouse and poured Grandma a large cup of tea to have with their toast. Reaching into the pantry for the jam, she turned to find Grandma at the table, getting her breath back, and adjusting the rather fetching sporty headband that was doing its best to hold in place her precarious pile of hair.

"Mmm, raspberry, my favourite," said Grandma, taking the jar and rummaging in her hair for a spoon. She gave it a quick wipe and began to generously dollop jam all over their toast. "What news, Red?"

Red had started opening the post. "Well, there's a letter from the library saying the new book we wanted is in and we can go and fetch it – oooh, can we go today, Grandma?"

Grandma nodded enthusiastically, munching a mouthful of toast.

"And our seed packets have arrived for the new variety of pumpkins we want to plant," continued Red. "Here's a postcard, but it's hard to make out who it's from. Snowy has nibbled the bottom, and it's a bit soggy." She tried to decipher the smeared and chewed writing. "As far as I can tell, it says: *From Russia, with love. Wish you were here.* Wait, it's from our neighbours, the Wolfes! That's nice, isn't it, they've gone on a family holiday. And what's this? Another mail order catalogue for leg warmers – Grandma, surely you don't need any *more* of those?" Red asked despairingly, looking down at the colourful knitted accessories round Grandma's ankles.

"You can never have too many leg warmers, dear," declared Grandma, slurping some tea. "And who's that from?" she said, indicating a mangled envelope, with rabbit tooth marks round a little bulge in the middle.

Red opened it and out tumbled a tiny parcel, padded for safety. She carefully unwrapped it, to reveal a small slender glass tube with a rubber bulb attached to the top.

"It's a pipette," said Red, holding it up. "How

strange. I've been looking for one of these for ages. I thought there'd be one in that old chemistry set upstairs, but no luck." She checked to see if there was anything else inside the envelope. "There's no note with it. Who could have sent us this, Grandma, and why?"

But Grandma was staring at the pipette. "Red," she said. "It's from your mother."

Chapter Two

Two days earlier, far far away, the president of a large country was stamping his feet. He was a deeply unpleasant man, with sausage-like fingers (which he liked to point and grab things with), and a flammable hairdo. His name was Harold Stump, and if he didn't get his own way immediately, he would stamp his feet until he did. And he was very much used to getting his own way.

He was with his advisers in his tower. Harold referred to them as his advisers, but to be honest, he didn't take much advice from them, as he rarely listened to anyone who made sense. Only the day before, he'd fired someone for suggesting that eating vegetables was good for you. On this day though, Harold was stamping his feet about the environment.

"Sir, we have acquired the most incredible piece of top secret information," began his chief adviser excitedly, gesturing to a sheet of paper on his clipboard. "With the utmost respect, we think it would be highly advisable to look at this data. The English scientist, Heather Clearwell, has spent several years researching solar energy and has made a major breakthrough. She's about to offer it to everyone in the whole world, but thanks to our spies, we're the first to hear about it, and we have the only known copy of the formula right here –"

"Pah!" shouted Harold, stamping his feet petulantly. "There are so many things wrong with that advice, I don't know where to start! Firstly, a scientist who is a WOMAN! Ha ha ha ha ha! That's the craziest thing

I've ever heard. Secondly, solar energy?! What's that when it's at home? I've never heard such nonsense."

"Well, sir, solar energy is where you get your power from the sun," said the second adviser tentatively. "It's supposedly a sustainable source and preferable to fossil fuel because –"

"Who owns it?" snapped Harold, pointing at them.

The advisers all looked at each other and shuffled their clipboards. The third adviser soothingly murmured, "Owns it, sir?"

"This power sun thing. Who owns it?" Harold repeated.

"Well, sir, it's, it's – it's the sun. Nobody actually *owns* it," stammered the chief adviser, perspiring.

"So it's for sale then? How much?" demanded the president, taking out his wallet.

"Er –" the chief adviser faltered. The room fell silent. Harold stamped his feet.

"HOW MUCH?" he roared.

The fourth, and most junior, adviser spoke up. "The sun is not for sale, sir. And besides, there's no need to attempt to buy it as we believe Heather Clearwell is going to offer her invention for free. It is the most wonderful opportunity." He began to get more impassioned. "Just imagine a world where there's no pollution or –"

"You're fired," shouted Harold, pointing at the fourth adviser. He wrenched the clipboard out of the chief adviser's hands, tore the sheet of top secret scientific data from it, scrumpled it up and tossed it in the bin. Which was made of solid gold. (Which made it very difficult for the cleaner to empty.) The president then flung the clipboard at the chief adviser's head. "Now, all of you, get out, and come back when you've got some good advice for me. I'm off to play golf. And win. I always win. I'm the best president ever."

Nobody dared mention that most of the president's golf balls ended up in the lake in the middle of the golf course, and this didn't count as winning, or make you the best president.

Instead, the advisers took one last look at the bin which now contained the precious piece of paper and all hurriedly left, grovelling their apologies.

As they closed the door behind them, they could hear Harold Stump saying to himself, "Female scientists! Pah! That's as likely as female presidents. No wonder her invention is free."

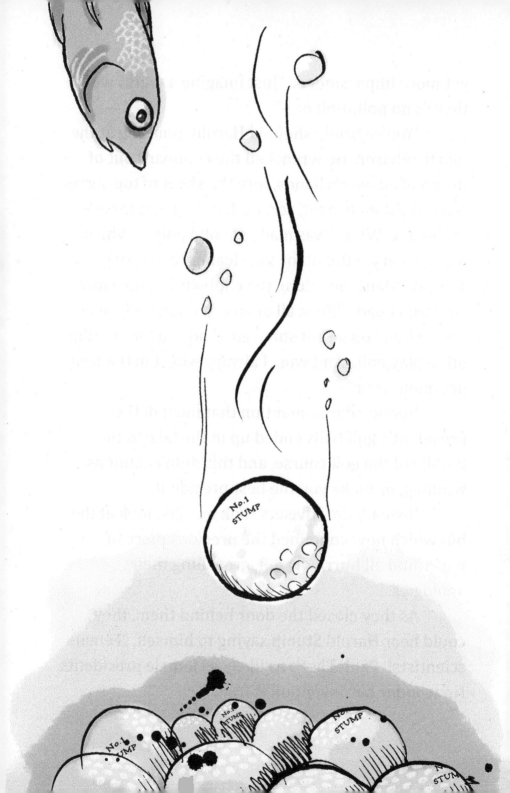

Crowding into the lift to take them to the ground floor, the chief adviser turned to the unfortunate fourth adviser and took the security badge from around his neck. "Sorry, Bert," he said (for that was his name). "It seems you've been stumped."

Rubbing the bump on his head, he addressed the others. "Gentlemen, to avoid being stumped ourselves, I advise that we steer well clear of this Heather Clearwell."

Chapter Three

As Grandma turned the pipette over and over in her hand, Red hardly dared to breathe. They very rarely spoke of her mother.

Suddenly, Grandma stood up, scraping the kitchen chair back, and decisively (but carefully) jammed the pipette into her hairdo.

"Red," she said. "There's no time to explain. Your mother is in danger. Run upstairs and fetch my cardigan and a catapult. We'll leave at once."

Red's eyes widened.

Grandma softened her tone and scooped her beloved granddaughter into a quick hug. "I know you have lots of questions. And I promise I will explain everything on the way. But there's no time to lose. Off you go. I need to get something from my trunk."

Grandma gave her a gentle push towards the stairs and, with a final lick of the spoon from the jam jar, vanished.

Chapter Four

As Bert was shown the door by burly security guards, the chief adviser had turned to the remaining second and third advisers and suggested a power lunch, over which they had better come up with some new advice for Harold. They headed towards the canteen, but the third adviser stopped and waved his clipboard.

"Silly me. I've left my pen in the president's office," he said. "I'll catch you up."

"Honestly, Simon," said the chief adviser to the third adviser (for that was his name). "Now is not a good time to be forgetting pens. Especially with the Oil Barons' Ball coming up at The Fancy Hotel. You know how excited the president gets. Do you realise how quickly you could be stumped for something like that? We're already a man short. And let's face it, Bert's advice was pretty good."

"Don't worry," said Simon. "Harold will be in his helicopter by now, on his way to the golf course. I'll just nip back up and fetch it and then meet you in the canteen."

The other two hurried off, contemplating how they could come up with some acceptable advice for Harold Stump, Best President Ever (and a man who had just thrown away something most sensible people would jump at), and wondering what was on the lunch menu.

Chapter Five

Grandma fastened the buttons on her cardigan, and made room in her hairdo for the catapult.

"Where are we going, Grandma? And how are we going to get there?" asked Red. "Travel dust? A new Go Glove? The umbrella left by that nice nanny when she last visited us?"

"No, dear. Something far more exciting. We're going to take the bus," replied Grandma. "Now, hold on tight and think of elephants and castles."

And with that, Grandma firmly clasped her granddaughter's hand and they both vanished.

When Red opened her eyes again, she took a moment to take in their new surroundings.

They were standing in the middle of the Elephant and Castle roundabout in London! She could hear her grandmother beside her, muttering about it not being quite what she had in mind, but suddenly Grandma stuck her arm out, and darted across the road, dodging traffic, and dragging Red behind her.

"Quick, Red," she cried. "The 148!"

They both sprinted to catch the double decker, just making it before it pulled away from the bus stop. Panting, Grandma reached into her hair for her Freedom Pass, and thanked the driver.

They went up to the top deck and managed to get two seats right at the front. Red looked out of the window at all the hurly-burly of city life around them and thought about this new adventure they were on, and what might happen. There were so many questions she wanted to ask!

Meanwhile, Grandma was restless in the seat next to her. She tapped her toes. She bit her fingernails. She took a crossword puzzle and a pencil from her hair and started to read out the clues. "*One across. The world's highest mountain. Seven letters.* What do you think that is, Red?"

"I think that's you avoiding talking about my mum, Grandma," said the little girl quietly.

Grandma paused over the puzzle, and then folded it up and pushed it back into her hair. She turned to face Red, relaxing slightly.

"You're right, my darling," she said, gazing at her. "Let's talk about your mother."

Chapter Six

Simon had got back into the crowded lift and pressed the button for the top floor. As they ascended, he listened to the very important people around him having very important conversations about all the very important meetings they were on their way to. They all ignored Simon.

Up and up they went, with the lift stopping at various floors to let people in and out, until finally it pinged to announce it could go no higher. He was alone.

As the doors slid open, Simon braced himself. If Harold Stump caught him going into his presidential office, he would be fired immediately. But he *had* to go back in there. He patted the pen-less clipboard dangling round his neck for reassurance.

To his left were the doors to the staircase that wound down through the whole building, and also up to the helipad above them. But straight ahead was a solid gold door with a nameplate that read:

HAROLD STUMP
BEST PRESIDENT
EVER

He walked over to it, trying to look nonchalant. By the lack of security guards, he could tell the president had indeed gone to play golf, but as Harold was known to change his mind quite rapidly, he could be back at any moment. For now though, all was quiet.

Simon took a deep breath and reached for the door handle. But as his hand closed around it, somebody else's hand landed on his shoulder!

He gasped and turned. It was Harold's hairdresser, Peg! She was a large jolly lady from Yorkshire, and naturally chatty. (Alas, Harold had great difficulty understanding her accent, so she limited herself to nodding and smiling at him during her daily challenge to mould his hair.)

She waggled a hefty can of hairspray at Simon. "Are yer going in there, pet? Could yer do us a right favour and put this in his desk drawer? It's a back-up in case I run out. I've never known anyone use so much. I'd do it meself but I'm late for a doctor's appointment, and they're like gold dust, aren't they. My flaming asthma is getting worse and worse. If I miss it, who knows when I'll be able to get another one."

Simon grasped the can. "Of course, no problem," he said quickly. Peg thanked him and hurried off.

Simon had another look round to check the coast was clear, and went into the office. It was strangely calm without the president in there, shouting and pointing. He took a moment to gaze at the sheer extravagance in the huge room.

Every possible endangered animal had their stuffed head mounted on the wall.

There was a coffee table made out of rhino horn, and a floor-to-ceiling bookcase made out of ivory. There were no books on the shelves, just golf trophies and pictures of the president pointing.

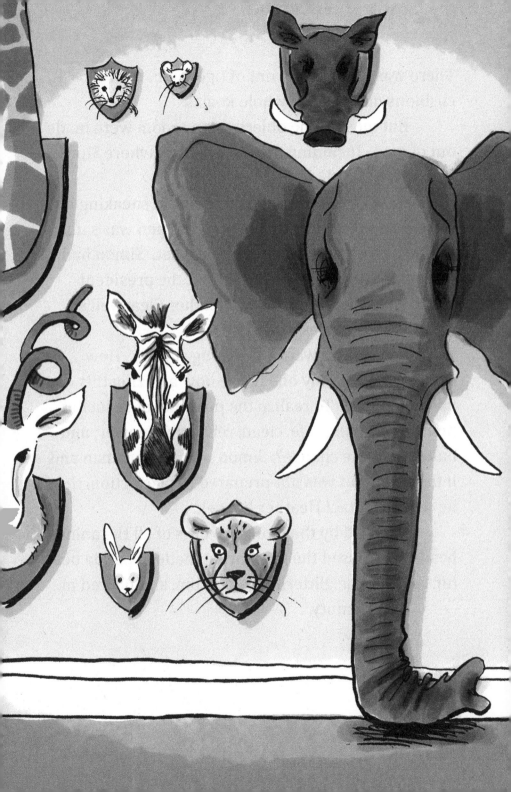

There was a sofa made out of tiger skin, with cushions made out of whole koalas.

But most of the objects in the room were made out of gold. Including the bin, which is where Simon was now headed.

He had not taken the huge risk of sneaking into the president's office for his pen. His pen was safely tucked away in his inside jacket pocket. Simon had come back to retrieve the data that the president had mindlessly tossed away. Heather Clearwell's invention for endless energy.

He crept forwards, sweating slightly. How could he be the only one to see how amazing this invention was? To realise the potential of reducing pollution; having safe, clean, renewable power; and halting climate change? Simon was a smart man and if the president was not prepared to take action, then he would contact Heather himself.

Watched by the mournful eyes of all the animal heads, he crossed the vast carpet made of panda bear fur, reached the glittering golden bin, and peered in.

It was empty.

Chapter Seven

The bus had halted at a zebra crossing. Grandma waited until it lumbered off again (the bus, not the zebra), then started to tell Red the story of her mother.

"Your mother – your brilliant, beloved, beautiful mother – is a scientist," she began. "She has spent most of her life trying to work out mysteries, and solve problems, and determine outcomes. Your great great-uncle gave her a chemistry set as a present on her eighth birthday, and she nearly blew up the treehouse. But, my goodness, she worked hard and got a lot better at experiments and by the time she left school, she was far cleverer than all her science teachers, and they could no longer answer her questions."

She smiled down at her granddaughter. "Clever like you, dear," she said, touching her gently on the nose. "Then a job offer came, in a laboratory. She was only sixteen, but it was such an opportunity for a promising young scientist, and I knew she had her heart set on it. I couldn't refuse her. Off she went."

Grandma paused and looked out of the window, giving a deep sigh. "Years passed and her work became more and more impressive. Oh, the discoveries she was making!" she continued. "It was at the lab that she met your father. He was a cleaner there. A nice enough chap, as far as I could tell, and they were very keen on each other, but unfortunately, he was rather clumsy and died in a hazardous waste mishap whilst she was pregnant with you."

Red was trying her best to absorb all this information. She looked up searchingly at her grandmother's face.

"Your mother loved you very, very much, Red," Grandma said softly. "But we both knew a science lab was no place to bring up a baby. She worked continuously and if she wasn't at the lab, then she'd be doing her research in the North Pole, or at the

Equator, or orbiting the Earth on the International Space Station, collecting data. And with your father gone, it was very difficult for her. So, right or wrong, you came to live with me in the treehouse. And I would send her a photograph of you, every month, and tell her all about you and how you were growing and what you were getting up to."

She paused again. "And what a wonderful, wonderful child you were." She smiled at Red, but then stared back out of the window. "And now she's in trouble."

Grandma reached into her hair for the pipette. "I made her promise to take this with her, from her first chemistry set, the one you play with, to use as a distress signal, just in case anything happened. It was a silly joke really, as she's more than capable of looking after herself, but now, after all these years, she's sent it."

Red's mind raced. "What kind of trouble is she in?" she asked.

"Your mother has worked on all sorts of remarkable projects, but her main focus was always on energy. And then a couple of months ago, she sent a message that her solar project was nearly finished and she was going to offer it to everybody for free. I can only assume that somebody found out about this and tried to stop her. There are a great many people in this world who prefer money to improving the state of the planet and nature."

Red sat in silence for a minute. It was an awful lot to take in, discovering her mother was not only a genius, but also in grave danger. She watched Grandma put the pipette that they had been sent back into her hair.

And then it came to her. The name scratched on the box of the chemistry set that she had played with for as far back as she could remember. How many times had she run her fingers over those letters? And when they had studied famous modern scientists at school, they had all sounded brilliant, but the whole class agreed one scientist had stood out as being *beyond* brilliant. It all came together in a flash.

"Grandma? Is my mother Heather Clearwell?

"Yes, dear. She is."

Chapter Eight

Simon gawped at the empty bin in despair. Curses! The cleaner, who hated lifting the golden bin because it was so heavy, had already been in and done just that. He thought quickly. There was still a chance the cleaner had the contents of the bin in his trolley. That's when he heard the whoosh of a helicopter landing on the roof outside.

Simon ran to the door and wrenched it open. Just in time to see the cleaner trundling the laden rubbish trolley into the lift. Simon called out, but the doors pinged closed and the lift began to slowly plummet to the basement.

There was not a moment to lose! He raced towards the doors leading to the stairs. He could hear Harold Stump on the other side, yelling (and no doubt pointing) at his pilot.

"All those rotating helicopter wing thingies blew my hair about when I got out! You're fired!" the president shouted.

There was nowhere to hide, so Simon shrank back against the wall... and the door slammed into his nose, as Harold barged it open. Ow ow ow ow ow!

With blood dripping down on to his clipboard,

Simon bit his fist to stop himself from whimpering. And realised he was still clutching the can of hairspray that Peg had asked him to leave in the desk drawer.

Stump stamped off into his office with his bodyguards, yelling at everyone in earshot. Simon stood dazed for a second, and then dashed out from behind the door, bleeding nose, hairspray and all, and started to run down 101 flights of stairs.

He had to reach the basement before the cleaner.

Chapter Nine

Finally, the lurching bus crossed the River Thames, making its way slowly over Westminster Bridge.

"Where are we going, Grandma?" asked Red.

Grandma pointed at the huge clock tower ahead of them. "There, my darling," she replied.

"Big Ben?" said Red.

"Yes, dear. Your mother's lab is underneath it. Ironically, she was never very good at being on time."

"My mother's lab is underneath Big Ben?" Red repeated incredulously.

"It was either that or Nelson's Column. The labs on the roof of the Science Museum were all taken. Press the bell, dear. We're getting off."

Chapter Ten

As Simon puffed and panted his way into the basement, he counted his lucky stars that at least he hadn't had to run UP the stairs. Still, 101 flights was quite a lot, and his legs were pretty wobbly. He made his way to the huge rubbish disposal area, deep underground, using the walls here and there for support. He turned a corner and his heart leapt. There was the cleaner's trolley! He wobbled over to it as fast as he could. But, oh no! It was empty!

DAILY NEWS.

YESTERDAY'S NEWS

The cleaner had dumped everything that had been in there, including the information on Heather's invention, somewhere in the huge mound of rubbish bags in front of him, all waiting to be taken away in lorries. It was a disaster!

There was only one thing for it. Simon put down the hairspray can he still held, wiped his sore and bloody nose, rolled up his sleeves, gritted his teeth, and prepared to delve deep. He would rummage through every last piece of rubbish until he found that data. Even if it took him all night.

Chapter Eleven

When Harold Stump dreamed at night, he dreamed of power. He loved many things: getting his own way; his celebrated hairdo; his solid gold teddy bear (which admittedly was rather uncomfortable to cuddle); and pointing.

But he loved power the most. Both the power that let him get his own way, and power from oil, the splendid slippery stuff that came magically from the ground and fuelled his cars and yachts and private jets.

Tomorrow night was his favourite event in the social calendar. An evening where he could preen and point and be adored by all the billionaires who loved oil as much as he did.

Tucked up in bed, wearing his polar bear fur onesie, with his hair safely protected inside a hairnet, he dreamed on. On the pillow next to him was his golden teddy bear.

And clutched in his stumpy sausage-like fingers was his precious ticket for the Oil Barons' Ball.

Chapter Twelve

The door to the lab was cleverly hidden at the back of the bell tower. As Red gazed up at the famous clock, Grandma pressed the buzzer and the door opened to reveal a spiral stone staircase.

Down they went, until they reached the lab; a cavernous room crammed with chemistry equipment and paraphernalia on every single bench and workspace.

In the middle stood Heather's assistant, a kind and clever scientist (with excellent hair) called Ashè. She had been sweeping up broken glass.

"Come in, come in," she called, rushing to greet them, and hugging Grandma. "I'm so glad you're here. And you must be Red," she said, holding her hand out. "I'd recognise you anywhere."

"Really?" said Red, shaking it. "How?"

Ashè turned and indicated the lab behind them. Three walls were covered with haphazard scientific charts and graphs and formulas and symbols and squiggles. But the fourth wall was covered with photographs. Of Red.

She stepped forward to take a closer look. Her mother had pinned up all the photos that Grandma had sent of Red every month over the years. There she was as a baby, wearing her first red hoodie. Learning to walk. Riding her scooter. Dancing at Kids Club with her friends. Paddling at the seaside with Grandma. Baking in the kitchen. Performing in shows at school with her classmates. Selfies with the Bookflaps Reading Club at the library. Watering the veg patch outside the treehouse. Playing with a chemistry set.

Behind her, Ashè handed Grandma a cup of tea. "I'm so sorry to tell you this, Grandma, but I was the one who sent you the pipette. Heather has been kidnapped. She'd just completed the invention, and it was such a wonderful moment we thought it would be nice to celebrate with some iced buns. So she was the only one here, as we'd popped out to fetch some. It's going to be very painful to watch, but the whole thing was captured on the lab CCTV. We have a camera in the corner for security. Unfortunately there's no sound on it, but we can clearly see what happened."

Grandma closed her eyes for a moment. Then she opened them, took a slurp of tea, and straightened her back. "Show me."

Chapter Thirteen

It *had* taken Simon all night to find that piece of
paper with the data on it. A night where he had
squelched his way through unspeakable things. He
had desperately unscrumpled thousands of sheets
of paper (most of them covered with gloopy, slimy
gunk), as he tackled the seemingly never-ending
mountain of waste. When he finally had the right
piece of paper in his hot, sticky hands, he was almost
too worn out to celebrate.

He had smoothed it out and carefully wiped
away something disgusting from a torn corner. He
could not believe he was the only one who saw the
true value of this amazing invention for endless
energy, and how greedily other governments would
jump on it. He'd gazed at it, and then tucked his
precious find behind all the other papers on his
clipboard, most of which were now soaked in goo,
and clipped his pen back in place.

Then Simon had called the lab and spoken
to Heather. He had told her he worked for one of
the most powerful leaders in the world. That his
job was to keep his ear to the ground and give the
best possible advice to the president, and that he

had heard about her invention. He told her that he would be able to advise her and help her unveil her pioneering creation. He said he was flying to London immediately and that she shouldn't speak to anyone else before he could see the work for himself. He had heaped praise upon her, and flattered her brilliant brain and tireless research.

Heather had believed him, and when Simon arrived the next day, with pear smeared on his forehead, a sticky lollipop stick stuck to his trousers, chewing gum in his hair, and several snotty tissues on the bottom of his left shoe, she had welcomed him in.

He told her he had first-class seats on the next flight out for them and that she should pack what she needed and they should leave at once. When Heather had questioned the need to hurry, he had begun to get agitated, and started gathering random bits of equipment. Heather, astonished and slightly alarmed, had asked him to stop. His agitation turned to rage. He shouted at her and called her names. Heather had been brought up to believe in good manners and had not appreciated his rudeness.

It was then that things took a turn for the worse. Simon threw a rack of test tubes across the room in a hissy fit and upturned several trays of iron filings. By the time he'd smashed a row of flasks and an evaporation dish, Heather told him to leave.

But it was too late.

He swore at her.

He threatened her.

And, as she reached for the phone to call for help, he hit her over the head with a tripod, knocking her unconscious.

It turned out Simon was not a nature-loving, sensitive peace-maker who cared about the environment. He was a devious, greedy, ruthless baddie.

Chapter Fourteen

Grandma watched the whole security tape in silence. At the part where the kidnapper had hit Heather, her eyes narrowed and her fist clenched so hard that she broke the handle off the teacup she was holding. The man on tape was then seen panicking. As he wildly looked around the lab, he spotted the camera in the corner and lunged at it to destroy the evidence. That was where the tape stopped... on a close-up of his face.

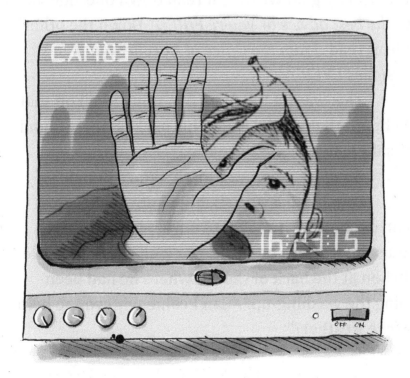

Grandma leaned in. "Gotcha," she whispered to the image. She then turned, grim-faced, to Ashè. "You were right to send me the pipette, dear. Thank you."

Red was trembling next to her grandmother. "Where has he taken her, Grandma?" she asked.

"Do not worry, my darling. She is absolutely fine and we are going to get her back," said Grandma firmly, hugging Red to her.

"There's not much to go on," said Ashè, holding up a pen. "This is our only clue."

She passed the pen to Grandma, who examined it. In brassy gold writing, it read down one side: *Give me the best advice or you're FIRED.* Down the other side, it read: *From the Office of Harold Stump, Best President EVER.*

"This was on the floor. We think it fell off that clipboard that he had round his neck. Bungle found it," said Ashè.

"Bungle?" said Grandma. "Who's Bungle?"

"I am," said a voice behind her. An eleven-year-old boy, with a mass of unruly red hair, and a thousand freckles on his nose, came out of the little kitchen at the back of the lab where he had been doing the washing-up. "Can I come with you to help rescue Heather?"

"Er, well, that's a very generous offer, Bungle," began Grandma. "But I think it's going to be rather dangerous and let's face it, we've only just met."

"Please can I come? Heather was always kind to me and she let me help out around here after school and in the holidays, doing the cleaning. I wanted to be here, because this is where my dad died when I was little," said the boy.

"I'm sorry to hear that," said Grandma, then stopped. "Wait, what? Your dad died here? Who was he?"

"He was the cleaner. He died in a tragic chemical waste accident nine years ago," explained Ashè. "He was rather clumsy, alas."

Red, who had been listening intently to all that had been going on, gasped.

"So, that means – that means – Grandma, what does that mean?" she stammered.

"It means, Red, well... it seems that Bungle is your half-brother."

Chapter Fifteen

In the lift on the way up to the top floor of the presidential tower, the chief adviser turned to the second adviser. "Have you seen Simon today?" he asked.

"No," replied the second adviser.

There was a pause.

"Oh. That pen must be proving very difficult to find."

Chapter Sixteen

Red and Bungle stared at each other. Could this be true? That they shared the same clumsy father who had perished in such an unfortunate way?

Red thought back to only that morning, when she had wondered what kind of day it was going to be. How her life had turned upside down since then! As she looked at the boy who had got to spend all that time with her mother, and to help out in the very lab that had been considered too dangerous for her to grow up in, she felt a huge wave of self-pity. Followed by a surge of fear for what had become of her mum. She wanted to weep with frustration and anger and jealousy and worry.

Grandma touched her gently on the shoulder. "Are you alright, dear?" she asked.

Red's thoughts swirled away from the lab and back to the amazing treehouse that was her home and the brilliant life she had there with her grandmother, who had taught her to be kind and generous and to share. What had life been like for Bungle, who had lost his dad? Where was *his* mum? And cleaning in a lab wasn't *that* much fun, surely?

Red swallowed. And took another look at

Bungle. Her half-brother. She nodded. "Yes, Grandma. I think we should get going. And take Bungle with us. And I think today of all days we need the ABC."

"That's my girl," said Grandma proudly. "Time to pay the office of Harold Stump a visit."

"Wait – we know the ABC," exclaimed Ashè, gesturing to Bungle. "Heather said it all the time. To be a) –"

"– adventurous!" shouted Grandma.

"– b) –" continued Ashè.

"– brave –" yelled Bungle.

"– and c) –" finished Ashè.

"– courageous!" cried Red. "Let's go and save the day!"

Chapter Seventeen

After a good night's sleep, Harold Stump was sitting behind his vast desk in his presidential office and pointing one of his sausage-like fingers at his chief adviser. "You," he said. "What advice have you got for me today? And make it snappy – I want to get my hair done so I look lovely and very important at the Oil Barons' Ball this evening."

The chief adviser adjusted his tie and gazed down at his clipboard. The words *climate change* in big red letters and underlined twice were top of the list, but he was afraid of being stumped. He decided to raise the next issue instead. "Well, sir, we thought we'd start with the funding problems for children's education. We'd advise you to –"

"Boring," interrupted Harold. "Move on! Move on!"

"Er, well, there's the homeless crisis –" the chief adviser said, scanning his long list.

"What? Just tell them to go home! Sorted!" cried Stump. "Next!"

The chief adviser gave a slight glance at the second adviser, and cleared his throat. "Then there's healthcare. Our advice is to –"

"Healthcare! *Finally,* something interesting. Let's go for a game of golf. That's healthy." He clicked his fingers for his clubs to be brought to him. "In fact, call China and challenge their president to a game. I bet I'd win. I always win," Harold crowed, getting to his feet and heading to the door. He stopped and turned and pointed at them suspiciously. "Where is everyone?"

"Pardon, sir?" said the second adviser.

"Why are there only two of you giving me advice?" he demanded.

"Well, sir, you fired –" began the chief adviser, but did not get very far. Stump had thrown a golf club at him.

"Humph," said the president. "Get me some more advisers. The best ones."

Chapter Eighteen

It is rarely acceptable to hit someone anywhere on their body, let alone over the head with a tripod, but Simon had found hitting Heather to be a terrible thing to do for a different reason.

He had never suspected she wouldn't automatically agree to come with him, and hadn't quite thought through a back-up plan. But after knocking her out and realising it had all been filmed, he went into panic overdrive. He was now faced with carrying an unconscious scientist and her invention up a spiral staircase. He also realised he didn't know what her invention actually looked like, or how large it was. He had to hope he hadn't already smashed it during his tantrum.

Simon reached for the sheet of data still attached to his filthy clipboard. The handwriting at the bottom described the outcome of the experiment, but he could not understand the scientific squiggles filling the rest of the page so it was of no help to him.

Rapidly filling his pockets with anything he could, he awkwardly hoisted poor Heather over his shoulder and headed up the stairs.

Chapter Nineteen

It was agreed that Ashè would stay and look after the lab. She printed out a screenshot of the close-up image of the man who had attacked Heather, and Grandma carefully stored it in her hair.

Then Grandma, Red and Bungle had all donned protective goggles (although it had taken a while to get Grandma's pair safely over her hairdo) and were ready to leave. They all hugged Ashè goodbye, and she wished them luck.

Grandma had decided that the best way to get to Harold Stump's office would be to travel by map. She had previously thought they would travel by spinach, but she hadn't brought enough for Bungle too. Travelling by map would be the fastest and safest way to go thousands of miles, and both children were excited because they'd seen it done before in films. She had taken a map from her hair and traced her finger along the route they needed to go.

With all three of them holding an edge of the parchment, Grandma had waggled her left elbow, done the map rap – which consisted of several verses of rapid rhyming slang, all of which she coped with admirably – and the lab had started to shudder.

Ashè stood well back and waved, as suddenly they were whisked off on their journey, magically travelling across an ocean to a large country far far away.

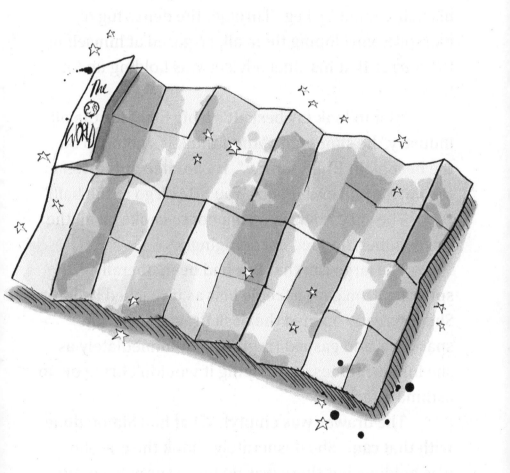

Chapter Twenty

In that large country, Harold Stump was back behind his desk, having played his fifth game of golf that week. (He won. He always won.) He was having his hair coiffed by Peg. Through the dense fug of hairspray enveloping them all, he gazed at himself in the mirror that his chief adviser was holding up for him.

"Got to look my best. It's a big night for the oil industry," he simpered. "And I think it's going to be the best night EVER for me." He pointed at himself in the mirror and exclaimed, "You SHALL go to the ball!"

The chief adviser, trying not to choke on all the sickly fumes, nodded encouragingly.

The large can that Peg had been liberally spraying from gave a feeble hiss as it reached its limit. She discreetly opened the desk drawer to get the spare can, and gasped (regretting it immediately as she inhaled fumes, and hoping it wouldn't bring on an asthma attack).

The drawer was empty! What had Simon done with that can? She desperately shook the one she was holding, but there was no more spray to spray. Peg was going to have to bluff it.

"There yer go, love," she said brightly, patting his hair. "All done, ready for yer big do tonight."

"What?" barked the president. "What are you saying?"

"Yer ready, pet. For yer big night out. Ooooh, yer look ever so nice."

"I can't understand a word you're saying," shouted Harold. "Stupid foreigners." He pointed to the chief adviser. "What's she on about?"

As Peg tried to signal to the chief adviser that there was no hairspray left and to please advise Harold that he was ready, the president clocked her in the mirror still in front of him.

He turned and grabbed the can from her in a fury and hurled it at the chief adviser's head. "How could you let this happen?" he snarled. "Do you know how important this evening is? You're worse than she is!"

Stinging from the blow, the chief adviser opened his mouth to reply, and wished he hadn't as billowing toxic gases swirled in. "Sir, with respect, she's used the whole can on you. I think your hair might be pretty well fixed," he choked.

"Oh, so now you're a hair expert, are you? Which is just as well, because your advice is always lousy. Make yourself useful and go and fetch some more hairspray. Immediately! The best one! Extra strength." Harold rounded on Peg and pointed at her. "And you're fired."

Chapter Twenty-One

Grandma turned the extensive menu over and over but could not find what she was looking for. They were in a café called the Pie Palace, recovering from their journey.

Red and Bungle sat quietly, sipping at some water; both of them excited but slightly shell-shocked. Neither could believe they had just crossed an entire ocean in a flash. And as Red sat next to her newly discovered older half-brother, she once again reflected on what a day it was turning out to be.

Grandma beckoned over a waiter. "Excuse me, dear," she said. "I'd like to order some pie, but I can't find the one I'm looking for."

The waiter politely pointed out the lengthy list of pies on offer. "We have apple pie, rhubarb pie, pecan pie, key lime pie, lemon meringue pie, cherry pie, berry pie, and pumpkin pie."

"Yes. I'd like some pea pie though. Do you have that?" Grandma asked.

"Pea pie?" said the waiter. "I don't believe we do, madam. But it's my first day working here. I could find out if they'll make you some," he offered.

"How thoughtful of you, dear. That would be

marvellous."

Red leaned forward. "Shall we just have some apple pie, Grandma? I don't know if they'll be able to make pea pie quite the way you like it. Plus, we should probably be on the move soon."

"You're right, my darling," conceded Grandma. She turned back to the waiter and handed him the menu. "We'll have three slices of apple pie and a pot of tea, please –" she peered closely at his name badge – "Bert."

Chapter Twenty-Two

When Simon arrived at the airport, he encountered his next problem. It was highly unlikely he would be allowed to take an unconscious woman on a plane. Even the taxi driver he had flagged down had eyed him suspiciously when he had bundled Heather into the vehicle and muttered that 'his wife' wasn't feeling very well and could they please hurry.

There was nothing for it; he would just have to wait for her to come round. Luckily they were in the perfect place to do this without arousing suspicion (because a highly-strung man covered in bits of rubbish and a woman who isn't moving can be highly suspicious) – Simon could say their flight was delayed if anyone questioned him.

Besides, now was a good time to come up with a plan.

As Heather sat slumped in a chair, he confided to her about how he was going to use her idea for a power source as a bargaining tool. He knew the president would be giving a speech at the Oil Barons' Ball that evening. And if he interrupted that speech and made one of his own, well, once all the billionaire oil barons had heard about this threat to their companies, they would make *him* president.

He went into intricate detail about how he would then start a bidding war and sell the invention to the company who offered the most money, and let them do what they liked with it. Whether they used it and made money from it, or whether they had it destroyed so it could never be used, he didn't care. His confidence in his scheme grew, and he drifted into a daydream about everything he would do when he was the most powerful man in the world.

Hours later, it dawned on him they'd missed the flight for which he'd bought very expensive tickets. He then realised he hadn't got Heather's passport. Curses! What was he going to do? He had to get them both to The Fancy Hotel to have his showdown with Harold and the oil barons. Who could he call in a favour from? And why was his thigh so itchy? He checked his pockets and made the scientific discovery that there'd been a chemical reaction from the things he'd snatched from the lab. A toxic concoction had burned through his trousers. Steam was rising. And an alarming rash had appeared on his leg.

Chapter Twenty-Three

Back at the Pie Palace, Grandma had gone for a wee. Red and Bungle sat awkwardly next to each other in their booth, and wondered what to talk about. How strange to suddenly find you had a half-sibling.

"So –" began Red.

"Do you –" started Bungle.

"Oh, sorry, you go."

"No, you first."

"I didn't really –"

"It's nothing."

Another uncomfortable silence fell. This is silly, thought Red. There are so many things I want to ask him. "What's my mum like?" she blurted out.

Bungle smiled. "Oh, she's ace. She's really kind. And she's super clever. I love her. We have lots of fun together."

Red prickled at this. "Oh. How nice for you."

"She taught me to ride a bike, and how to do Sudoku, and how to change a fuse," he continued.

"Couldn't you have done those things with your own mum? I don't see why you had to hog mine," said Red petulantly.

"I wasn't hogging yours. I do lots of things with

my mum. She's a writer. She's really cool. And she's happy for me to be friends with Heather. She knew my dad – *our* dad – was having a baby with her, and she'd be really happy to know I have a sister. Even a grouchy one." He jostled her elbow playfully, but Red moved away from him.

"Whatever. I bet she's not cool. Being a writer sounds boring. And *our* dad doesn't sound very nice, going round having lots of babies with different people."

"She's an awesome writer! I don't know what you're so cross about. My mum and dad split up when I was two. I don't remember him. But Mum told me he worked at the lab, which is why I wanted to be there. You know, after school and that."

"Sounds like you haven't got any mates," sneered Red.

"Sounds like you're jealous," retorted Bungle.

"Sounds like you're an idiot," finished Red, pulling her hoodie up and crossing her arms.

Bungle humphed, and turned away and picked up a nearby newspaper.

Suddenly, Grandma appeared back at the table. "How are you two getting on?" She eyed Red, who was sitting pointedly angled away from her brother.

"Have you been having a nice chat?"

Red glared at Grandma, who remained unruffled. "It's quite a surprise for you both. And it takes a while to adjust to new siblings. I should know. When I was on tour with The Beatles in the sixties, and found out *my* half-brother was – ooooh, here comes Bert with our pie."

As Bert served the pie, Bungle looked up from the newspaper. "We're searching for the president, aren't we, Grandma? Because of the pen I found in the lab."

"What a great detective you are," muttered Red sullenly.

Grandma reached over and gently took Red's hood down. "That's right, dear," she said to Bungle, giving Red a chiding glance.

Bungle indicated the headline. "Well, it says

here that he's attending the Oil Barons' Ball tonight at The Fancy Hotel. We could go there! He might know where Heather is. Or she might even be there!"

Grandma stiffened and took the newspaper from him. "The Oil Barons' Ball? That sounds like just the ticket. Well done, Bungle!"

This was too much for Red. "Oh, it's not fair," she cried. "He got to spend all that time with my mum, and now he's getting all the praise for thinking where she might be! I hate him!" She burst into tears.

Bungle flushed, and looked like he was on the verge of tears himself. And then he spoke up. "Do you know the one place in the lab I wasn't allowed to clean? Do you? Go on, have a guess."

"I don't know! And I don't care!" sobbed Red.

"Well, I'll have a guess, dear," piped up Grandma. "Was it the hazardous waste area? I certainly hope so, seeing as what happened to your father," she added, under her breath.

"No," said Bungle. "It was the wall of pictures. All the pictures of YOU, Red. Your mum may have been long-distance, but she talked about you all the time." He stopped and considered this. "Well, she mainly talked about science stuff, but after that, she talked about you. And whenever she got stuck on a formula, or an invention, or an equation, she would go and gaze at those pictures and always come up with the answer. She said you were her inspiration."

This set Red off crying harder than ever.

"Scoot round and sit with me, my darling. I need a cuddle," said Grandma, taking a tissue out of her hairdo. She realised it was quite snotty, and put it back.

Bert, hovering with cutlery, solicitously offered Red a napkin as she ran round the table and squished in next to her grandmother.

"That's better," said Grandma. "Now, let's dry those eyes. We're a team, remember, and all on the same side. Pie might help. Tuck in."

Bungle had already finished his slice. He leaned forward. "Red, would it also help to hear the story of how my dad – *our* dad – died? You know, to kind of clear things up?"

Red bit her lip, as her heaving sobs subsided. *Would* it help to hear this? She thought for a moment. "Grandma and Ashè said it was a chemical waste mishap. It sounds awful."

"Yes," said Bungle. "He was cleaning some of the hazardous materials up one day, ready for safe disposal. As he helped the driver load the barrels onto the collection vehicle outside the lab, he dropped one. It rolled off, into the road. Our dad ran after it and got hit by a bus."

"Oh no!" sniffled Red. "And then he died!"

"No," said Bungle. "He was taken to hospital with a broken right arm, ribs, and collar bone. They put what they could in plaster. But as he was leaving, he tripped and fell down the stairs."

"Oh no!" exclaimed Grandma. "And then he died?"

"No," continued Bungle. "He broke his right leg. They took him back in and plastered that too. But as he sat on the ward waiting to be discharged, he knocked the hairdryer that the lady in the next bed was using into a bowl of water that he was soaking his swollen left foot in, and electrocuted himself."

"Oh no!" said Bert, who was still standing there. "And *then* he died?"

"No. They decided it was safer to keep him in hospital. Unfortunately he caught an infection and died the next day."

"Oh," said Grandma, through a mouthful of pie. "I'd kind of imagined he'd fallen into a vat of chemicals." She paused. "Still, our poor beleaguered

NHS."

"Grandma! Our poor *dad*!" said Red.

"Yes, dear. Indeed. So... does that make you feel a bit better?"

Red looked uncertainly at Bungle. Then pushed her plate of pie nearer to him so they could share it. "Strangely, it kind of does."

Bert regarded his customers. "You folks seem to be having quite a day. Is there anything I can do to assist? I couldn't help overhearing you're looking for the president. I used to work for Harold Stump, so I know a bit about him."

All three diners stared at him.

"Goodness me, Bert, what a coincidence," said Grandma. "Please take a seat. We need all the help we can get."

Chapter Twenty-Four

The ballroom at The Fancy Hotel was packed to the rafters with very, very rich people. Champagne and fancy canapés were being circulated on fancy trays, as socialites and celebrities mingled with oil barons. Photographers and reporters roamed, taking pictures and getting interviews.

In the middle of the room was an ostentatious centrepiece – a giant gold sculpture of an oil rig, which was pumping real oil up and out like a chocolate fountain. Several film stars, an elderly politician, and a waiter had already been slightly splattered and were now giving it a wide berth.

They were all awaiting the grand entrance of the president. Who was half-an-hour late. The chief adviser and the second adviser were trying to coax him out of the men's toilets, where he was fussing with his hair in front of the mirror. It was already so stiff with all the hairspray on it that it looked like a helmet, but Harold was not happy.

"You look wonderful, sir. Are you ready? It's time to give your big speech," said the chief adviser, anxiously checking his watch and hoping nothing would be thrown at him.

"I can't give my speech until my hair is perfect!" screamed Harold. "This is a very important night!" He pointed at his advisers and stamped his feet. "You'd better find me the best hairdresser ever! Now!"

The advisers hastily left the room.

"Bert would know what to do," sighed the second adviser.

"Yeah. Bert was great."

Chapter Twenty-Five

Everyone in the booth had listened as Bert recounted the tale of his job as fourth adviser to the president, and how he had been stumped. When Bungle had shown him the pen he'd found in the lab, Bert was shocked. And when Grandma had taken the picture of the kidnapper out of her hair, he was horrified to see the face of his former colleague, Simon, the president's third adviser, and realised he must have gone back for the data.

Bert instantly pledged to help save the day. He had then come up with an elaborate plan to get them all into The Fancy Hotel.

"... and we abseil onto the roof and disguise ourselves. As chambermaids. We could hire costumes. And make fake IDs. And hide in laundry baskets and get carried in through the trade entrance and then jump out. We must hurry!"

He leapt up and looked at Grandma, expectantly.

"You've been watching too many films, dear." And with that, she laid out some coins to pay for the pie, clasped his hand, nodded to Red and Bungle to also join hands with them, and they all vanished.

Chapter Twenty-Six

After frantically emptying his pockets, dousing his leg in water, and ripping a large hole in his trousers to ventilate his scorched skin, Simon had called Harold Stump's personal pilot. It was a long shot but he thought if he could bribe him, he might be able to use one of the president's many private jets.

It turned out the pilot was available, having been fired yesterday, but demanded a high price for taking such a risk. That high price was everything Simon owned, including his house, all his money, and his collection of rubber chickens.

It would all be worth it, Simon thought. With Heather's invention, he would be rich beyond his wildest dreams.

The pilot flew over, picked them up, and flew back. They were on their way to The Fancy Hotel at last.

And as the plane came in to land, Heather fluttered her eyelids and gave a slight groan. She was awake.

Chapter Twenty-Seven

When Bert next opened *his* eyes, he was standing with Grandma, Red and Bungle beside the oil rig centrepiece in the middle of the ballroom at The Fancy Hotel. He blinked several times in disbelief and staggered backwards. "What the...? How did...? What just happened?" he said, flabbergasted.

Bungle gave him a reassuring pat. "You get used to it. Ish."

Grandma was eyeing the oil rig. "Thank heavens we didn't land on top of that monstrosity," she murmured, moving away before it bespattered her, and helping herself to a vol-au-vent from a passing waiter.

Several society ladies (and one oil baron) in extremely expensive (and expansive) frocks were giving Grandma's cardigan, velour tracksuit, and leg warmers very snooty looks, but Grandma had no qualms about making her own fashion statement and fluffed up her hair, imperiously. She withdrew the picture of Simon and handed it to Red. "Keep a close eye out for him, my darling," she said. "Oh, and Bert? You've got oil all over your trousers, dear."

It was at that moment that the chief adviser

and the second adviser spotted Grandma across the crowded floor. They had come to frantically search for somebody to help them prise Harold Stump out of the toilets. Billionaire oil barons were already tapping their watches and beginning to burble 'time is money' and other such nonsense. The advisers made their way through the hordes.

"Excuse me, madam," said the chief adviser. "We couldn't help but notice what a fabulous hairdo you have, and we wondered if you might assist us with a rather delicate situation. You appear to be a very capable lady and we would appreciate your help."

Grandma raised an eyebrow as they explained their predicament. "It would be my pleasure," she told them, then turned to Red and Bungle. "You two stay here with – oooh, that's going to stain, can you help him with all that oil? I don't think the Pie Palace will be wanting that uniform back, dear," she said, indicating Bert who, having just about recovered from his travel experience, was bent double, dabbing at the oily mess on his trouser hems. She gestured to the door. "Shall we, gentlemen?"

Grandma grandly accompanied the advisers through the fancy foyer. But as they neared the toilets, her hair bristled. She sensed her daughter, and she sensed danger.

She paused outside the door, and smiled tightly at the security guards posted there (along with the long queue of men who weren't allowed in while the president was hogging the facilities. These men were jigging up and down with anxious bladders).

"Just give me two minutes alone with Harold," said Grandma.

The advisers gave each other a look, and nodded. As she shut the door behind her, they heard her tell the president, still preening by the mirror, "Hello, dear. I've come to give you some advice."

Chapter Twenty-Eight

A waitress approached Bert and Red and Bungle, who, despite sticking out like sore thumbs amongst all the finery, were doing their best to mingle.

"Evenin', all. Do any of yer fancy a drink?" she asked them, in a familiar Yorkshire accent.

Bert stared at the waitress. "Peg? Is that you?"

Peg had not wasted much time since being fired. The former hairdresser to Harold Stump had taken a job as a waitress the very same day.

"Bert! Eh oop! It's dead nice to see yer! I heard *you'd* been fired an' all. What a day! But where are my manners? I didn't know you had kids," she said, smiling at Red and Bungle.

"Ah, they're not mine, Peg." He leaned in. "We're here on a mission. Red's mum has been kidnapped and we're trying to find her. She's got the most amazing idea for clean renewable energy. Can you imagine a world with no pollution? Honestly, it's a work of pure genius, I think she might have solved the –"

"It's a long story, Peg," Red interrupted. "Basically, we came here because we think the man who took my mum might try and use her invention to make some sort of demand from all these oil barons and the president."

"Ooooh, that's cracking detective work. Aren't you clever," said Peg. "You obviously take after yer mam."

Red blushed. "Actually, it was Bungle's idea," she admitted.

Peg looked from one to the other. "Well, I can see you make a right good team."

Red unfolded the picture of the kidnapper and held it up. "Have you seen this man?" she asked.

"Yeah," Peg replied. "And I wish I'd given him a piece of my mind, an' all. Why've you got a picture of Simon?" She peered closer. "And why's he covered in slime? Actually, don't answer that. Serves him right."

"That's just it. Simon is the man who kidnapped Red's mum," said Bert.

"Ooooh, that's shocking! I always thought he were right shady. Heaven knows what he's done with that flaming spare hairspray. Wait 'til I get my hands on him," said Peg. "What can I do to help? The manager here's a right moaner, but I'll do what I can. 'I don't pay you to stand around making small talk,' he told me, even though I were far from making small talk, and –"

"What are you doing?" hissed the nasty manager, standing right behind her. "I don't pay you to stand around making small talk!" He shoved a tray into her hands. "There are thirsty people here, very *important* thirsty people. Get a move on." He glared at the children and Bert, and steered Peg away from them.

Peg mouthed as she was led away, "I'll keep me eyes peeled! Good luck!"

Chapter Twenty-Nine

It must be said that Heather Clearwell had never been the most sociable person in the room. Nor was she very good at reading human behaviour. Her logical mind was always trying to work out the right answers and, as we know, people do not always behave the way they should.

When Simon had come to her lab in London, she had been pleased to welcome him. When she had come round in another country after being hit on the head with a tripod, she had not been as pleased, but she was still prepared to give him the benefit of the doubt.

However, after spending half an hour cooped up in a taxi with the man, on their way from the airport to the hotel, she was beginning to tire of him. He was rehearsing his speech over and over, which outlined his plan. Heather found it to be a rather complicated and long-winded plan, but thought it best not to mention it. Besides, Simon barely let her get a word in edgeways. She wondered what Ashè had done since finding her missing, and whether the attack had been caught on camera.

As Simon droned on and on about world

domination, her thoughts drifted to molecular equations, and she took comfort in calculating prime numbers. By the time they had pulled up outside the hotel, she had the beginnings of an idea for a device that could suck all the plastic out of the oceans and was idly wondering what all that plastic could be turned into.

Chapter Thirty

Grandma left the toilets, closing the door behind her, and gave the waiting group of men another tight smile.

"Gentlemen," she said. "Harold has asked *me* to give his speech this evening. Shall we get started?"

The two advisers looked at each other. Whatever Grandma said in the speech, it was bound to make more sense than anything Harold would ever say. They shrugged.

"After you, Grandma," said the chief adviser, bowing slightly and gesturing back towards the ballroom.

They led her to the brightly lit podium which had a big group of photographers kneeling in front of it, all waiting to take pictures of the president. She tapped the microphone with her finger, sending a reverberation round the room. "Testing, testing," she boomed. Everyone fell silent, and all eyes turned to Grandma.

"Ladies and gentlemen," she began, addressing the entire audience. She sought out Red and Bungle. "Girls and boys," she smiled. "President Stump has asked me to give his speech tonight. And I can safely say –"

But whatever it was she was about to safely say, she never got to say it. Harold Stump, Best President Ever, came roaring into the ballroom.

"GRANDMA!" he yelled, pointing and stamping his feet like never before.

The crowd gave an almighty collective gasp at the sight of their president. A shocked hush descended. Until the sound of a little girl laughing broke the silence. It was Red. She couldn't believe what her brilliant grandmother had done.

Harold Stump's prized hairdo had been dyed purple and shaved into a mohawk.

It was so good to laugh, after all the strains and worries of the day. After a moment, Bungle joined in. They laughed and laughed, clutching their sides and each other for support.

And one by one, the whole room began laughing too. They all pointed at the president, and laughed at him. Apart from the photographers, who all frantically clicked their cameras, instantly sending thousands of pictures out into the world.

This was the last straw. Harold barged through his formerly loyal supporters, grabbing at anyone in his path, blustering for all he was worth, and heading for Grandma. "You're all fired! You're all fired! Especially you, Grandma! YOU'RE FIRED!"

"No, Stump! YOU'RE fired!" shouted a voice from the door.

Everyone gasped again and turned. It was Simon, still covered in rubbish (and scratching his now-blistering leg), gripping a still groggy Heather.

Grandma's hair bristled and sent out a burst of sparks.

"What?" said Harold, trying to put a name to the rather dirty face of his third adviser. "What are you talking about?"

"I'm going to be the president! Me! Me!" babbled Simon. "Because of the invention thing! And my great plan! All the oil barons will make me president!"

This was confusing to everybody, not just Harold, and a puzzled mutter rippled round the room.

"Oh, for heaven's sake," said Heather. "Should I clarify the situation? Simon kidnapped me so he could use my invention. It's all part of his, er, great plan."

"Who are you?" asked a nearby oil baron.

"I'm Heather Clearwell," she said.

"She's an amazing scientist," called out Bert.

"She's my friend," shouted Bungle.

"She's my daughter," declared Grandma fiercely, so close to the microphone that it echoed round the huge ballroom.

"She's my mum," said Red softly.

The crowd gasped one last time, and parted to reveal the little girl in the red hoodie.

"Red?" said Heather. "Is that you?" She pulled away from Simon.

"Yes. Hello... Mum."

They stared at each other across the room.

"No, no, no, no, NO!" howled Harold. "This is NOT the way this evening is supposed to go! Kidnapping and sappy reunions? Pah! That's even worse than female scientists!" He strode towards the podium, pointing. "Where are my advisers?" He grabbed a tray from a nearby waitress and flung it at the chief adviser's head. But the second adviser reached out and deftly caught the tray.

"No," he said. "Enough." He threw it back at the president, hitting him right on the nose.

"Ow!" cried Stump. "That hurt!"

"Not as much as this will, pet," said the waitress – Peg, of course – giving him a colossal kick up the bum. "Right nice handiwork, by the way, Grandma," she said, indicating Harold's new hairdo.

"What's that? What's she saying?" Harold whimpered, clutching his bottom.

"Oh, shut up," said Peg, kicking him again.

It was all too much for Harold. He wished he was tucked up in bed with his golden teddy bear. All he could do was stamp his feet. He stamped and stamped and stamped. Unfortunately, he was quite near the oil rig centrepiece. And the more he stamped, the more the oil splattered... then streamed... then gushed.

People nearby began to get soaked. An oil baron tried to move away, and slipped. He grabbed at the giant shoulder pads on the frock of a society lady

to try and steady himself, but she screamed and
whopped him with her handbag. She too then
slipped in the oil and, flailing around, slapped the
man next to her. He thought it was somebody else,
and turned and clouted the man next to him. Who
then turned and thumped the man next to *him*.
The fight did not take long to escalate.
The more people got covered in oil,
the more slippery the floor
became, and the
more people were
grabbing each other
to try and stay
upright, the more
they ended up
whacking each
other, and
falling over.
It was chaos.
Soon everybody
in the room
was involved.
Grandma had
an heiress in
a headlock.

Bert was biting a bigwig. Bungle was battling an old battle-axe. Peg managed to give the moaning manager a swift smack with her tray. The chief adviser pummelled a chief executive and the second adviser clobbered a chairman with a chair.

Only Red and Heather stood untouched in the middle, gazing at each other.

Harold Stump surveyed the carnage of what was supposed to be the best night ever, and gave one final stamp of his feet on the shiny ballroom floor. Which turned out to be his biggest mistake.

He slipped.

For a moment he windmilled, thrashing and floundering, his arms flapping desperately, and his stumpy fingers reached out to grab something to save himself.

He caught hold of the clipboard round the chief adviser's neck. "Help me, you fool," he yelled, teetering and sliding in the oil.

The chief adviser considered Stump for a moment. Then he reached up and untied the clipboard's ribbon from around his neck.

"With pleasure, sir. Here's my advice," he said, and let go. Which meant there was nothing left for Harold to hang on to.

Down he went, with a bang and a splat.

"Oops," said the chief adviser. "He appears to be out cold."

"Yes, dear," replied Grandma. "I advise you let him have a little lie down for a moment."

Simon did a jig of victory. "President down! President down! He's no longer fit to preside!" he gibbered. "Which means *I'm* the new president! Let me hear you all say it!"

"Don't be ridiculous," replied Grandma, rolling her eyes. "And if Harold weren't flat out on the floor, I'm sure he would say, 'You're fired'."

"Yes, the game's up, Simon. You're going to prison," said Bert.

"Then you leave me no choice! I'll destroy THIS!" he cried, holding up his clipboard.

"A clipboard?" said the shoulder-padded society lady.

"No, no, *this*!" he said, waving the piece of paper he had gone to such lengths to get. "I know for a fact there is no back-up copy!"

Heather turned to look. "You're right, there is no back-up copy."

"I'll do it! I'll destroy it!" shrieked Simon hysterically.

"No!" shouted Bert.

"No!" shouted the press.

"No!" shouted all the oil barons, piled up on top of each other, but not actually understanding what they were saying 'no' to.

Red spoke up. "Go on then. Destroy it, Simon. Heather... my mum... will recreate it. Nasty, greedy, selfish bullies should not rule countries," she said calmly.

"Actually, I hate to disappoint anyone expecting a dramatic ending, but that's my shopping list," said Heather. "The formula for the invention is written on the wall in the lab." She looked at Red. "All the important things are on my walls there."

Simon gaped at the page in his hand. "But... but... but it's got all these squiggles on it! And there's a picture of the sun! And it says at the bottom: *scientific outcome: endless energy – offer this for free to everybody*!"

"Yes, I like to doodle on my shopping lists," said Heather airily. "But those squiggles are just my shorthand. Bungle can confirm that. Read it out, Bungle."

Bungle looked at Heather, and raised an eyebrow. "Er...?"

"Go on," said Heather, nodding.

"It says... let me just make this out... it says, 'Pea soup, er, iced buns, erm, loo roll'. Oh, and 'More tape to stick up photos of Red'."

"That's right, Bungle. Spot on."

"Noooooooooooooooooo!" screamed Simon. A shopping list?! All that effort for *a shopping list*? He'd better make a run for it. His plan had gone horribly wrong, and these people were clearly mad. Plus the oil barons were glaring at him and shaking their heads angrily. There was nobody on his side. It was all over.

He held up the sheet of paper, and ripped it into shreds. The fragments fluttered to the floor.

Then he turned and scarpered. As fast as his fizzing

leg could carry him. The burly security guards closed in to try and stop him, but slipped and went down in a pile of hulking muscle.

Simon was going to get away.

Grandma, however, had other ideas. She narrowed her eyes and, as she stepped forward, Red did a double take. Grandma was wearing REALLY BIG PANTS over her tracksuit!

Red watched in amazement as her grandmother whooshed along the glossy floor like an ice-skating champion, reaching Simon as he fled into the foyer.

"Just give me a moment, everybody," she said, rolling her sleeves up, and shutting the door behind her.

Chapter Thirty-One

Everybody in the ballroom leaned in to listen, and then shrank back as thumps and whumps and several *hi-yaaaaaaaa*s could be heard, along with impressive karate kicks and desperate wails from Simon.

After a minute, Grandma opened the door. Simon was on the floor behind her, tied up with leg warmers.

"That's better," she said, dusting off her hands. "Now, remember, everybody – violence is never the answer."

Heather had picked up some of the tiny shreds of paper, sticky with oil, and was staring at them.

Bungle collected some scraps to pass to her. "I'm sorry, Heather. I tried to think of what might be on an actual shopping list."

"You did very well, Bungle. My plan didn't work, that's all. It's not your fault."

Grandma looked at Heather and the scraps. "That *was* the invention, wasn't it, dear."

"Yes. It was my first attempt at a double bluff. I'll stick to science from now on. But I think I can recreate the invention. It won't take long. Maybe a year," said Heather.

Red gasped. "I don't understand. You tried to fool Simon into thinking that *wasn't* the formula? Why would you risk it?"

"It's exactly like you said, Red," replied Heather. "Nasty bullies should not rule countries."

Harold Stump chose this moment to come round. "Oooooh, my head. What happened?" he groaned feebly, attempting to sit up. He poked at the oil on his clothes. "What's all this gloop?"

The press all gathered closer, expectantly.

"Hello, dear," Grandma said to him. "You've had a little nap. How many fingers am I holding up? Can you see two? Good. Now, can you remember your name?"

"Yes, of course, it's errrr, I think – er, oh, I'm, er," he began. "Is it, errr –"

"That's right, dear," said Grandma brightly. "Your name's Errr-old. And this here is Bert," she said, indicating him. "And you've had Bert declared president. Haven't you, dear," she stated.

"I declared Bert president?" wondered Harold. "Errrr, yes, I guess that's right."

All the press instantly wrote this down and started taking pictures of Bert.

"Over here, Mr President! Smile for the camera,

Mr President!" they called. "Can you tell us what your first act as president will be, sir?"

Bert looked at Grandma. She nodded at him. "Go ahead, dear," she murmured. "You will make an excellent president."

Bert drew himself up, proudly. "My first act will be to fund Heather Clearwell's invention for solar energy. This means she will be able to have it ready much sooner. And I would advise all the oil barons here to get on board with this incredible technology immediately. It's a new dawn for this country, and the state of the world."

The press all scurried out of the room to flash this big story round the globe.

The oil barons all hurried out too, slipping and sliding as they went, reaching for their phones to organise meetings with each other.

All the other guests trooped out, contemplating how they would ever get all the oil out of their hair.

The moaning manager surveyed the giant oil slick, and went to take a job at the Pie Palace.

The chief adviser and second adviser held their hands out to Bert.

"Congratulations, Mr President," said the chief adviser. "We think you'll do a wonderful job."

"Thank you," replied Bert. "Can I offer you both posts as my advisers?"

"Actually, we've been discussing a change of career. Our last piece of advice: you should offer this lady the job as your adviser," said the now-former chief adviser, smiling at Peg. "She'll be right champion." He then turned to the now-former second adviser. "Philip," he said (for that was his name). "Shall we go and open a dance studio in Rome? Or a bookshop? Or a bakery?"

"Yes," said Philip. "All three."

"Ooooooh, that sounds dead nice," said Peg. "My first bit of advice for the president is that we come and visit yer. Ta-ra, boys. Can yer do us a favour on yer way out? Drop Simon off at the police station." They all turned to look at Simon, still trussed up, with pear on his forehead. "Possibly via a doctor. His leg seems to be oozing summat dead nasty. Then he's going to prison, and I know just the job for him in there. He can be in charge of sorting the rubbish."

"No! Please no! I'll do anything!" said Simon.

Peg held her finger up. "Zip it, buster. I advise nobody listens to owt Simon says." She paused. "I never liked that game."

"I've been waiting all day to do a 'Simon says' gag!" said Heather.

Everybody groaned, but Red laughed and patted her mum's arm. "*I thought that was funny.*"

"Thanks, Red," she said.

Still slumped on the floor, Harold Stump scratched his purple mohawk. "What is it that *I* do? What's my job?"

"Oh, you're a *very* important person. With a *very* important job," said Red.

"Yes," finished Bungle. "You work on a golf course, fishing old golf balls out of the lake."

Grandma was tucking into a sandwich that she'd taken from her hairdo. "Perfect," she said through a mouthful, putting an arm round the boy. "Are you hungry, dear?" she asked, offering him a bite.

Chapter Thirty-Two

Bert granted them all the privilege of flying home on the presidential plane. "What a remarkable family. Thank you. I'd accompany you, but I've got a lot to do getting this country in shape." He exchanged details with Heather so they could arrange plans for her invention, then gave them a heartfelt salute.

The flight home was a strange one. On board Heather got straight back to work, hunched over a notepad, scribbling endless squiggles.

"She's not coming home with us, is she, Grandma. Even after she recreates the invention," said Red sadly.

Grandma slipped her hand into Red's. "No, my darling. She'll go back to the lab. But we can visit her. And we'll take iced buns."

Red thought this over. She gazed up into the eyes of her beloved grandmother, and squeezed her hand. "Okay," she said. "Iced buns it is." Then she stopped and looked her grandmother up and down. She was still wearing the really big pants.

"Grandma, were those pants what you fetched from your trunk before we set out this morning?"

"Yes, dear," replied Grandma. "You know I'm

partial to a superhero costume."

Red eyed the oversized undies, and decided to leave it at that. But then paused. "Why did you want me to bring the catapult?" she asked.

"I thought it might make a nice present for Bungle. Don't you?"

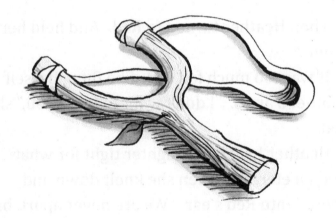

Chapter Thirty-Three

Back in London, Grandma and Heather huddled together. Red watched as Grandma took the pipette from her hair and handed it back to her daughter. "Just in case, my darling," she said, with a smile. She kissed her forehead and they said goodbye to each other.

Then Heather turned to Red. And held her hand out.

It was too much for Red. She flung herself into her mother's arms. "I don't want to leave you," she sobbed.

Heather held her daughter tight for what seemed an eternity. Then she knelt down and whispered into Red's ear. "We are never apart, baby. Know this." She stroked Red's cheek, and dried her tears. "I love you."

Red's lip trembled. "I love you too –" she savoured the unfamiliar word – "Mum." Then the little girl bravely straightened her back, in the style of Grandma. "Now, go and save the world."

Bungle gently tapped Red's arm. "You okay?" he asked.

She nodded, and gave him the catapult. "Come

and visit us soon," she said quietly. "I'd be really sad to lose you."

He smiled at her, and wrapped her in a giant hug. "You're not going to lose me, sis. I'd love to come and visit. And I can always do with help in the kitchen in the laboratory, you know. Your mum doesn't half drink a lot of tea."

Red thought for a moment. "Maybe YOUR mum could write a story about our adventure? I'm sorry I was mean about her. Being a writer is really cool."

"Being a scientist is really cool too," replied Bungle, nudging his sister. "We've both got cool mums."

"Yes. And a cool dad," added Red.

"Yeah. Clumsy, but cool."

Chapter Thirty-Four

It was dark as Grandma and Red walked up the path to the treehouse, but glowing fireflies danced round Grandma's hair, lighting their way.

Red thought back over the adventure they'd had since the post had arrived that morning, and what a day it had turned out to be.

She gasped. "Grandma! We didn't go to the library!"

"Never mind, dear. There's always tomorrow."

Chapter One

Norma Dimble had worked in Flappington Library for forty-seven years. She had started as a junior assistant to old Mr Tibbs back in the day when library books had little tickets inside, and had to be date-stamped to be borrowed.

Other colleagues had come and gone, but Norma loved nothing more than books and when Mr Tibbs retired at the age of 104, she finally became the head librarian.

Now, two minutes before opening time, she stood by her desk with the key to the door in her hand and surveyed the space around her. There were books, of course. But also a row of computers. A photocopier. A rack of DVDs. Giant colourful cushions on the floor of the children's room.

It was so quiet you could hear a pin drop. Even the clock ticked in silence.

As Norma's eyes travelled over the books, neatly arranged in alphabetical order on the shelves, she felt a sense of pride. Amongst the various activities that would be taking place that day were Bookflaps (the children's reading club), the OAP Rap Writing Performance Poetry Club, and the support group for collectors of rubber chickens. Flappington Library would be filled with people of all ages, colours, shapes and sizes, bringing noise and life to the building.

Norma watched the clock reach the hour and nodded to herself. She headed to the door and unlocked it. It was going to be a very important day.

Chapter Two

It was just after eleven o'clock when Grandma and Red zoomed into the library. Rusty Buildup, the caretaker, was up a wobbly ladder outside the front door with an assortment of paint pots and a large paintbrush.

"Morning, Rusty," called Grandma. "How's your back today?"

"Oh, not so bad, thank you, Grandma," he replied. "Lots of odd jobs to get done around the place though. I'm just giving the door a nice fresh coat of paint."

Red could see her friends in the children's room, already gathered for their weekly Bookflaps reading club. Two of her best friends waved at her through the large glass doors separating the area. These two friends were Benoit, a very excitable French boy with big brown eyes, and Gig, a clever girl with lots of curly hair and really cool glasses. Gig was deaf and wore hearing aids, but was also a skilled lip reader and had been using sign language from a very young age. Red loved discussing books with them, and had been having fun learning French with Benoit, and to sign with Gig.

She gave Grandma a kiss on the cheek and skipped off to join the club. "Laters, Grandma."

"Indeed. Laters, Red," replied Grandma. "I'll be waiting for you in an hour. And you be careful up that ladder, Rusty. I'll bring you out a cup of tea. You look like you've earned one."

The children's room was packed, with everybody all talking about the book they had been reading that week. Nadia, who ran the club and was also the mum of Zainab, Fatima and Mierna, three of Red's school friends, was handing out sheets of paper. As well as discussing the books they read, Nadia encouraged them to write their own stories and to design artwork which they displayed on the walls.

"Before we begin, I'd like to introduce a new member of our group, Beatrix Bloom. I know you'll all be very welcoming, and that she's going to have a great time with us," she said.

Beatrix waved at everyone and beamed a big smile, and they all chorused hello to her.

"Now," continued Nadia, "as well as our thoughts on this week's book, there's a special project I want us to work on. I'm going to divide you into teams and you're going to design a poster for the upcoming short story competition. We'll put all the posters up, but there's only room for one on the main noticeboard, so make it enticing! Remember, there are two separate categories – one for children, and one for grown-ups, and the winning stories will be published in the local newspaper. Red, do you think Grandma will be entering this year? We all know how much she loves stories."

"Oh, I'm sure she will," said Red. "We know a witch on roller skates who wants to enter too. And I'll tell my neighbour, Edwin – he's really into stories now."

"Excellent. Okay, the teams are: Alex, with Tess, Mabel, Liv, Zainab and Beatrix. You're all going to be on the table in the corner." Those children all ran to sit down.

Nadia then pointed to another table. "Naomi's team will have Jack, Firdaws, Harry, Oliver and Betty. This is your space here."

Standing by the third table, Nadia called out, "Hebe! Your team will be on this table. You'll have Yaqub, Isabella, Stan, Mierna and Mason." Hebe and her team all rushed to take their places.

Finally, Nadia turned to the remaining children. "So that leaves Red, Benoit, Gig, Cosmo, Maeve and Fatima. You're going to be on the cushions, down here. Team captains, come and get your pens to share. Let's get crafty!"

Chapter Three

Grandma was sitting beside Norma's desk. They were both having a cup of tea, and sorting through donated food bank items and dividing them into categories.

"Mmmm," slurped Grandma. "Nothing like a good cup of tea, dear."

"Yes, Grandma," replied Norma, watching the clock. "Lovely."

"I've so enjoyed reading the book choice this week. I'm looking forward to discussing it. I particularly relished the grisly crime in Chapter Three," said Grandma. She was part of the adults' reading club, the Dusty Jackets, who met on Tuesdays.

"Yes, Grandma," replied Norma, checking her watch. "Lovely."

Grandma observed the preoccupied librarian for a moment. "I'm flying to the moon this afternoon," she said.

"Yes, Grandma," replied Norma, looking back at the clock. "Lovely."

"Norma!" said Grandma. "You're ever so distracted today! Shall I leave you in peace, dear? I can go and check my emails on the computers or something."

"Oh, I'm sorry, Grandma. You're right, I *am* distracted today. I've got a lot on my mind."

"Is there anything I can help with?" asked Grandma. "We've known each other for a long time; I'm always happy to listen."

"Thank you, Grandma. But I think this is something that –"

They were interrupted by a clatter outside and a shout from Rusty.

"Oi! Watch where you're going! I nearly fell off my ladder!"

In the doorway stood three people in suits, casting an ominous shadow. Hookem, Bodge and Curdle.

Chapter Four

A friendly rivalry had broken out in the children's room, as the teams started on their posters.

Alex was urging his team to consider dinosaurs, after a recent visit to the Natural History Museum. "Everyone loves dinosaurs," he said, wielding a felt-tip. "If we draw a really big one, people will be inspired to write stories. Our poster will definitely be the best."

Meanwhile, Naomi, artistic as ever, had gone for a cut-out design, and everyone at her table was busy snipping.

Hebe's team was squabbling over the glue and several of them already had their fingers stuck together.

Red, Benoit, Gig, Maeve, Cosmo and Fatima were discussing their options.

"I sink we should do eet like zis," said Benoit, sketching out a possibility. "'Ow does it look like?"

Red considered his sketch, and tapped Gig's shoulder. She pointed to the picture and held her thumb up questioningly. Gig shook her head and picked up a pencil, quickly outlining *her* idea. It was going to take a lot of diplomacy for them all to decide on how best to design their poster.

Back at Alex's table, roaring and laughter erupted. Their dinosaur was now on a surfboard and eating fudge but, as Red knew, anything could happen in a story.

Chapter Five

As Hookem, Bodge and Curdle approached the desk, Grandma's hair let out a tiny shower of warning sparks.

"Good morning, ladies," said Hookem, consulting a folder he was carrying. "We've come to measure up."

Norma hastily got to her feet. "Oh, ah, er, yes, Mr Hookem," she said, rushing round the desk. "Let me show you the area."

"There's no need for that, Miss Dimble," piped up Bodge. "We can see it all clearly from here." He turned and gazed round the room. "Nice high ceilings."

"Yes," added Curdle coldly, revealing an assortment of measuring tapes about his person and selecting an industrial-looking one. He pulled the strip of tape measure from its case, and let it snap back with a threatening thwack. "Don't let us disturb you. We'll just start with this bookshelf right here," he said, turning to the nearest one.

"Okay, yes – wait, what?" said Norma. "Why would you measure the shelves?"

"Yes, gentlemen. Why WOULD you measure

the shelves?" asked Grandma, looking at Bodge and Curdle, who had already set to work.

"Didn't you know, madam?" said Hookem. "We're clearing all these old books out. This library is the new storage space for our company. *Someone –*" and here he glared at Bodge – "leant on the 0 button on the computer whilst doing the stationery order, and bought 80,000,000 rolls of packing tape."

"Sorry, boss," mumbled Bodge, swiftly moving on to measure another shelf.

"So, as you can imagine, we need a storage facility for the excess packing tape we now have. And these shelves will be perfect, once we've got rid of the books. We won't take up any more of your morning. I can see how busy you are," Hookem finished, with a sneering nod at the tins of beans lined up in front of Grandma.

"No, but wait!" cried Norma. (Although not very loudly. She never raised her voice in the library.) "It's only the social area and the computers and the DVD display section that are going!"

"I'm afraid not, Miss Dimble. This whole place is deemed a 'social area'. *Everything* is going." He stared through the glass into the children's room and smirked. "Particularly everything in there." He sauntered off to join Bodge and Curdle. "That's right, boys. Keep measuring."

Behind Norma, Grandma stood up. "Oh, Norma. What have you done?"

Chapter Six

Back in the children's room, Red was having problems of her own. Benoit and Gig were still arguing over the design for their poster, and Cosmo, one of the younger members of their team, had got bored, given up completely, and eaten a crayon.

"Eet ees eempossible to do zis," cried Benoit, throwing his hands up in the air. "We must 'ave ze poster to be like zis!" He began to speak in rapid French, only half of which Red could understand.

Gig, meanwhile, had switched to even more rapid sign language to communicate with Red; describing plans for bold lettering and a striking colour palette.

As Red's eyes followed the flashing fingers, and her ears filled with French, she began to think that perhaps surfing dinosaurs were the way forward.

Chapter Seven

Norma and Grandma watched Hookem, Bodge and Curdle criss-cross the library with their measuring tapes. Nothing was left unmeasured.

"Grandma. I've made an awful mistake," Norma confessed. "If old Mr Tibbs knew, he'd put me in the Defaced Books Box."

"I don't understand, Norma. Tell me why you would contemplate even a *section* of the library being wasted like this?"

"Because look around you! Look around you, Grandma! A library is a place for books! Books! Not giant cushions, and computers, and heaven knows what else. It should be a place of calm, a tranquil haven, where the only sound should be the 'sssssssh' of a librarian! I could just about accept audiobooks, but everything else... clubs, courses, baby dance classes, games nights, language lessons, this group, that group – I could go on and on! I mean, only last week we had a theatre company in, performing in the children's room! A theatre company! In a library! Two grown women, dressed in nightwear and prancing around – some ridiculous yarn about a genie chopping down trees! And the noise the children in the audience made! Shrieks and claps and laughter! Honestly – in a library!" For the first time ever, Norma raised her voice. "A LIBRARY!"

"It sounds rather good," replied Grandma. "I wish I'd seen it."

"The children should be here to take books out. Books!"

"Well, did the children take books out afterwards?"

"Yes. But that's not the point."

"But Norma, look what you've done. In trying to get rid of the computers and a comfy place to sit, you've also got rid of all your beloved books."

Norma groaned. "I thought they would just put a nice stationery cupboard in that area, for a few rolls of packing tape. And I was going to use the rental money they were offering to buy some large-print DIY books for the self-help section. Heaven knows Rusty could do with some."

"Alright," said Grandma. "Let's try and settle this in a civilised manner."

She strode over to the men. "Mr Hookem, I'm afraid there's been a misunderstanding. The offer to use a small section of this library as a storage facility has been withdrawn. We would kindly ask you to honour this, and to stop measuring things. Including me," she added, as Bodge ran a ruler down her back, and wrote down his findings. "Perhaps you could simply cancel the order for the excess packing tape? That seems to be a perfectly sensible solution."

At that moment, Rusty, with his paintbrush clenched between his teeth, came through the door backwards, trundling a porter's trolley.

"Ernnh, Nuhmuh?" he called, as he tried to manoeuvre it in, bashing the walls on either side. "Nnnneh nuh nuuuuhgh nuheee nnuhnnuh, nnh nnh nnnh nnnnh."

Everyone looked at each other.

"Could you say that again, please?" asked Norma.

Rusty took the paintbrush out of his mouth and repeated himself. "There's a huge lorry outside, full of this stuff." He awkwardly steered the trolley round, accidentally knocking the door shut in the process, to reveal it was precariously

laden with packing tape. "And the driver, Marge, says she's got orders to start shipping out all the books, once the tape is unloaded. What's going on?"

Norma gasped. "No! No! What have I done? I shall chain myself to a shelf!"

"Oooh, I think I've got some handcuffs in here somewhere – we could use those. Hold on," said Grandma, rummaging through her hair.

"Don't waste your energy, ladies," said Hookem, condescendingly. "Or your handcuffs. The shelves are staying. It's just these useless books that are going. All of them."

"*Useless?*" Grandma, Norma and Rusty cried in unison. That did it.

Grandma rolled up her sleeves.

Rusty rolled the trolley over his own foot, and yelped.

And Norma unleashed a battle cry, the loudest sound she had ever made in the library – or anywhere else. She raced across the room and grabbed the paintbrush from Rusty, then advanced on Hookem, brandishing it. "Get out of this library, you nasty man! You'll never take these books!"

"Our company policy is to take threats of physical violence *very* seriously. I'm calling for back-up," blustered Hookem, backing into the DVD display.

"Rusty, lock the front door!" shouted Grandma.

"Way ahead of you, G'ma. It should've been left propped open to dry, but that bloomin' trolley put paid to that. The wet paint will have sealed the door shut by now. We're all stuck in here."

There was a pause as this news sunk in... ending when Norma clonked Hookem with the paintbrush. "No 'back-up' for you, then. Take that!"

Curdle came hurtling from the tiny staff kitchen, where he had been measuring the kitchen sink, to defend his colleague. Rusty stepped in to block his path and the two of them began to tussle, sending rolls of tape flying.

Grandma's hair bristled as she assessed the situation. She was more than capable of taking care of these baddies who were threatening the library, but Rusty needed help. Despite still relying on his mother to tie his shoelaces, Curdle was fighting dirty and Rusty was not handy when it came to fisticuffs. And Bodge was nowhere to be seen.

Grandma glanced through the glass into the children's room. Gig was laughing uproariously at somebody's joke and caught Grandma's eye. The little girl waved happily at her.

Grandma smiled. A Bookflaps army!

She began to sign to Gig, quickly but clearly explaining what she wanted the children to do. Gig watched carefully and nodded, before turning to alert Red.

The fight was on.

Chapter Eight

Curdle had easily overcome Rusty and tied the poor caretaker's hands together with a fabric measuring tape. He'd shoved a book in his mouth for good measure, and rolled him under a shelf.

Norma had been swiping at Hookem with the paintbrush as though her life depended on it, splattering paint over his expensive suit. He had run to the door and tried to wrench it open, but it was indeed stuck fast. She chased him round the library, making more noise than she had ever made in her entire life.

Grandma thought it was probably good for Norma to be getting things out of her system, and let her get on with it. But when Curdle joined the chase and cornered Norma, she prepared to take action, and dropped into an expert karate stance.

This was when they heard the rumble... the stampede of dozens of little-to-really-quite-big feet approaching.

"Chaaaaaaaaaaaarge!" yelled the whole Bookflaps army, as the children tore into the main library.

They were followed by Nadia, who rushed to help Rusty.

The children swarmed throughout the space, whooping and bellowing. Some of them descended on Hookem, who pleaded for mercy as they walloped and biffed him. Naomi landed a mighty punch and Hebe scored a swift kick on his shin, as Grandma turned a blind eye.

But in the mayhem, Curdle managed to grab Norma and hold her captive.

"Right, you horrible kids," he shouted. "None of you move, or the librarian gets it! This is what's going to happen. When I say so, you're all going to start piling these stupid books by the door. And no funny business! We've come here to fill this building with packing tape, and that's exactly what we're going to do. Hookem, come and hold Miss Dimble. The rest of you – sssssh! Let's have silence in the library! Ha ha ha!"

Hookem, bedraggled and whimpering, shook himself free of the children, including Cosmo who was tenaciously biting his ankle, and made his way over to Norma. "I hate kids," he snivelled. "Even more than I hate books! I'm especially glad *your* ridiculous room will be crammed with packing tape!"

Which is when Red had an idea. The children were spread out everywhere. She called out in French: "Benoit? *Où es-tu?*"

His reply came from over the other side of the library, by the abandoned trolley. *"Ici*, Red, *ici!"*

This was exactly what Red wanted to hear. She started to give him instructions – in French.

Hookem and Curdle looked at each other in alarm, and then at Red.

"Stop that! What are you saying? What's that language?" said Hookem.

Unbeknownst to them, Red had told Benoit to pass rolls of packing tape to each member of the book club.

And prepare to strike.

As Hookem and Curdle both made their way menacingly towards Red, they were swooped upon by a throng of angry children, armed with tape. And thanks to all their craft activities, they knew exactly what to do with that tape.

In a matter of minutes, both men were tightly parcelled up like Egyptian mummies, their arms wrapped tightly to their sides and their legs bound together. Then the children took great pleasure in taping them to each other, back to back.

Hookem hollered and Curdle cursed, until Grandma, proudly supervising, gave Red the nod.

Red ripped off a piece of tape and passed it to Gig who stuck it over Hookem's mouth. And then she ripped off another piece of tape and passed it to Benoit, who stuck it over Curdle's mouth with a flourish.

"Silence in ze library, *non?*" he said. *"Voila!"*

Maeve broke into an impressive impromptu street dance in celebration, cheered on by all.

Chapter Nine

"Well done, gang!" said Grandma. "There's nothing like teamwork."

"Hold on," said Norma, quickly recovering from her ordeal. "What about the other one? Bodge?"

"Oh, and where's Beatrix?" said Alex, scanning all the faces. "She's on my team, but I can't see her."

Everybody rushed to check behind each shelf and search all the areas.

Until Red stopped and pointed through the glass into the children's room. "There they are," she exclaimed. "Look."

Bodge and Beatrix were sitting on a cushion with a book. She was reading it to him.

They all ran into the room.

"What's going on? Beatrix, are you okay?" asked Grandma.

"Yes, I'm fine," she said. "I'm reading Mr Bodge a story. He reminds me of my Pops."

Bodge looked up, his eyes shining. "This is such a wonderful book! I remember it from when I was a boy. It was my favourite story. Beatrix has been reading it to me."

Grandma and Norma glanced at each other.

"Well, that's nice," said Norma.

"I feel sad that we ever tried to get rid of all the books in here. I'm so sorry. I'm going to make sure all that packing tape gets returned."

"Er, well, some of the packing tape has just been used, actually," admitted Grandma.

"Well, *most* of the tape then," said Bodge.

"That would be very kind of you," said Norma graciously.

Beatrix looked at Bodge, and then at Norma. "Can Mr Bodge join our book club?" she asked.

"That's a lovely suggestion, Beatrix. Mr Bodge is possibly a little bit old for Bookflaps, but he's more than welcome to join our Dusty Jackets group for grown-ups." Norma paused. "And there are a great many other clubs and classes available here at the library, which I'd be more than happy to tell him about."

"I've got a suggestion too," said Nadia. "Why don't we ask Mr Bodge if he'd like to choose which poster goes on the noticeboard for us?"

"Zat is ze good suggestion," cried Benoit. "I sink ours will be ze one, *non*?"

All the teams scrambled to fetch their posters to present to Bodge, including the incredibly sticky glue-based one.

There was lots of excited pushing and shoving and clamour, but when it came down to it, the dinosaur was a clear-cut winner.

Chapter Ten

The hour was up. It was time to go. Besides, the OAP Rap Writing Performance Poetry Club would be arriving soon, and they were notoriously touchy about being kept waiting.

"Hmmm. What will prise that door open?" Grandma reached into her hair for an old bread knife, then ran it round the seal. She stood back and gave the door a hefty kick. "There we go. Freedom," she declared. "Although you'll need to repaint, I'm afraid, Rusty."

Norma patted Grandma's arm. "That's not a problem, Grandma," she said. "Rusty and I are going to make Flappington Library fabulous. You've all convinced me that a great library isn't just a place for books, but a place for people to come together and do a variety of wonderful things."

Bodge bundled Hookem and Curdle, still parcelled up and looking very sorry for themselves, into the back of the lorry. He swung himself up into the cab, as Marge revved the engine, ready to return the packing tape.

Everybody gathered on the pavement to wave goodbye, and Bodge proudly flaunted his new library card and a copy of the book for discussion at Tuesday's Dusty Jackets meeting.

"It's a whodunnit. Look out for the gardener in Chapter Three," called Grandma. "He's decidedly shifty."

"Grandma!" Bodge shouted, as they drove off with a honk of the horn, "No spoilers!"

Chapter Eleven

"We'd better get going, Red," said Grandma. She had taken a sandwich from her hair and was eating it. "I really *am* flying to the moon this afternoon. When I was an astronaut with Neil Armstrong, we would always – oh, would you like a bite, dear?" She offered the sandwich to Benoit, standing beside her.

"*Non, merci, Grand-mère*," he replied, wagging a finger at her. "*Mais bon appétit.*"

Red hugged her friends goodbye.

"*Au revoir, Rouge*," said Benoit, ever the joker, as Gig and Red rolled their eyes and blew raspberries at him.

Grandma saluted Norma. "You're a wonderful librarian, dear. The people of Flappington are lucky to have you," she told her. "And old Mr Tibbs would be very proud. Oh, and have a go at some rap writing. I think you'd be very good at it."

Grandma and Red headed back to their treehouse, both of them carrying treasured library books to start reading later.

"Grandma, I've just realised!" said Red. "You weren't wearing your really big pants to fight the baddies!"

Grandma smiled. "Well spotted, dear. We'll just have to have another adventure then, won't we?"

Over to you...

A story within a bedtime story about a boy who thinks he can't write stories; a girl wondering what sort of day it will be; and a library holding a short story competition were *our* starting points - can YOU write an adventure for Grandma and Red? We'd love to read *your* stories!

Would you like to design some artwork for the walls of Flappington Library? Get crafty!

Heather in *STUMPED!* has got the beginnings of an idea for an invention that will suck all the plastic out of the oceans and turn it into something useful. Can you think of what that might be? Or come up with a whole new invention!

And how many 'suddenlies' are in this book? Can you count them all?

Do send your stories, art, feedback, ideas and sandwiches to us. Plus there are activity sheets and resource packs on our website. And come and see Grandma and Red live in action (before our knees pack up) – either in a venue near you or at your school!

reallybigpants.co.uk
childrenstheatre@reallybigpants.co.uk
Twitter: @reallybptheatre
Facebook: Really Big Pants Theatre

Acknowledgements

In March 2015 we performed *SUDDENLY...!* on World Book Day at Avondale Park Primary, a school just a couple of miles down the road from our HQ in London. The audience absolutely rocked, and we returned the following year to perform another show. Then in June 2017, a fire changed the local community forever. Some of the children who died in Grenfell Tower that night had been part of our amazing audience at Avondale Park. We wanted to include the names of these children, along with the mother of one of the families, who worked at the school, and their siblings, as part of the Bookflaps club in *SHELVED!*. It is only a tiny gesture, but we hope in our own way to mark their all-too-short lives.

A REALLY BIG THANK YOU TO:

Rosie Alabaster, artist extraordinaire. Talented, resourceful, and downright fabulous. Totally calm in the face of a zillion *"Could you just..."*'s and rogue indents. We recommend you get your hands on a copy of her picture book, *DADDY WAS A ROCK STAR* – it's a masterpiece.

Philip Joel (champion choreographer and scratchcard aficionado), Maya McAllister Demangeat (film-maker and all-round wonder), Joseph Degnan, Strathmore Publishing, Orphans Press, Dave Morritt of D Sound, Julius Waters, Lee Wemyss, Teresa Gallagher, Alison Steadman, and Mark Williams.

All the audiences who have come to see Really Big Pants' shows – WOW. Children *and* grown-ups, you've all been ace. Come again!

All the schools we've performed in, and the teachers who work SOOOO hard – here is an apple for you:

All the teams in theatres, arts centres, museums and all the other creative spaces we play in, who book us, and then look after us so well. All the lit fests, libraries and gorgeous bookshops – especially Chicken & Frog Bookshop – long may your pages turn.

Beanstalk, a lovely reading charity that we are proud to have partnered with on several projects, and all the other literacy organisations doing wonderful work.

My oldies, the BEST OLDIES EVER.

My sister, Jane, for always manning the helpline and who will appreciate the Oil Barons' Ball.

All the pesky kids who call me Auntie Joe (amongst other things). You need to read the book to find out if you got a mention.

Laydee, Girl on the Back Row, and Ros Povey – my fellow AOY prima ballerinas – for nawteeness, Yorkshire chat, and pring yangs. And grammar. The raspberry jam is for you.

Naomi Gane (aka Pam), lover of books, lip gloss and roundabouts, who will also appreciate the Oil Barons' Ball.

Peter Davidson (yes then, Daaaar-ling, I think you'll find), Robert Hamilton, Claudine Harbour, Sophie Hallett, the Stacksters, Stevie Mol, Sturdy, and Lynch.

Laura Anderson-Ford, née Bannerman, who wanted to write a children's book for her beloved daughter, Grace. Banners died in 2016, aged just 39.

But most of all to Willow Nash – partner-in-pants, the left leg to my right (I'm always right), and the finest Health & Safety Officer a company could ever wish for. For all the times we laughed so hard we nearly called ourselves Pelvic Flaw, I salute you.